TO FIND A KILLER

Micah knew it would be best not to look at his wife and son as the train pulled out, but of course he had to look. They stood on the station platform, expressions sad and maybe, in Alice's case, also angry.

He waved at them, trying to make himself smile through the dirty window, and only vaguely succeeding. He didn't feel like smiling. He wanted to weep aloud.

He didn't know why he was doing this . . . didn't even know exactly what he was doing. All he knew was that he had to go to Colorado, and try to find a phantom from his past.

And then . . .

There's where it grew murky. What would he do if he did find Barth? Preach to him? Say a prayer with him? Give him a Bible?

Kill him?

It was a possibility. God help him, it was indeed a possibility.

Other *Leisure* Books by Will Cade:
LARIMONT
THE GALLOWSMAN
FLEE THE DEVIL

Genesis Rider

WILL CADE

LEISURE BOOKS  NEW YORK CITY

To Rhonda

A LEISURE BOOK®

October 2000

Published by

Dorchester Publishing Co., Inc.
276 Fifth Avenue
New York, NY 10001

ISBN 0-8439-4785-3

Printed in the United States of America.

Genesis Rider

Chapter One

Skinner's Hill, California, 1851

Twenty years before, a boyhood accident with a log auger had cost Leroy Barth his right eye. As he shoved his bearded and sweating face close to that of Micah Ward, that dead eye was an ugly, ruined pucker that held Micah's gaze against his will.

The other eye, the good one, squinted at him, boring into him like a sort of auger itself.

"See this blind eye of mine, boy?" Barth growled, his breath like molded cheese in Micah's nostrils. "Know what that eye sees?"

Micah swallowed, pulling back, terrified. But

Barth's grip was strong and held him.

"That eye sees nothing, boy. Not a thing. The same as your eyes seen that night at the old cabin. You know the night I'm talking about?"

Micah nodded. His throat was very dry.

"Tell what you seen that night, boy."

"Nothing . . . nothing."

"That's right. Nothing. Just like this dead eye of mine. Did you see my brother there, boy?"

"Yes."

Barth shook him. "You answer me again! Did you see my brother?"

"No . . . no. I saw nothing."

"That's right. You didn't see him at all. Not a thing. And when they set your rump on that testifying chair and ask you that same question, you'll give that very same answer."

Micah was afraid he was going to faint. He was ten years old, but just now felt as if he was hardly more than a baby, too scared even to cry.

"You seen nothing at all of my brother that night. Not hide nor hair. Right?"

"Right . . ."

"You seen no fight, no knife, no man killed."

Micah stared at the dead eye, fighting tears. Barth shook him. "No man killed! Say it!"

"No man killed."

Barth smiled and nodded, still gripping Micah's shoulders tightly. "There's the boy! The boy who seen nothing, and who'll tell nothing! The boy who don't remember." He paused, then let go of Micah's right shoulder. Reaching down, he brought up a knife out of a sheath at his belt. He waved it menacingly under Micah's nose. "See that, boy? That's the thing that will make you keep on being the boy who don't remember."

Barth picked the end of the knife into the soft flesh beneath Micah's right eye. "See this eye of mine? Feel it? If you get in that witnessing chair and all at once decide that you did see something that night, and if you tell, I'll give you an eye just like mine. No, two of them. I'll cut your eyes right out of your head . . . you understand me?"

Micah couldn't squelch tears now. He nodded.

Barth picked him with the knife again, breaking the skin a little. "Only difference will be, you'll have two eyes like mine, not just one. I'll blind you, boy. I'll blind you. And I'll kill that momma of yours, too. I'll do it, and don't think I'm lying."

Micah was afraid he might faint and collapse. He had no doubt that Leroy Barth would do everything he threatened, and more.

Barth made a sudden grunting sound, moving the knife and making a quick thrust. Micah sucked in his breath and tried not to scream as Barth inflicted a small but painful cut straight down along his left jawline, then another horizontal one at the top. "There we go . . . my brother's initial. A nice T right there on your face.

It's just a reminder, boy. Just a reminder of all you didn't see, and all you won't tell when they put my brother on trial."

Barth let Micah go at last. The boy stumbled back and fell on his rump. Blood ran down the left side of his neck. Micah looked around, hoping he might see someone else who'd witnessed what Barth had just done to him. But this was an isolated hollow, thick with trees. No one else was around.

"I'll kill your pappy, too, for good measure," Barth said coldly, sheathing the knife. "You remember all I told you, boy. And you keep your mouth shut. Not a word of what has happened here today to nobody. You tell your parents, and I'll know. I'll come cut your eyes out if you breathe so much as a word. You understand me?"

Micah nodded.

Leroy Barth stared down at him, then laughed with contempt. He turned and strode away.

Micah waited until he was gone before he allowed himself to break down completely. Rising, he ran, sobbing, deeper into the woods, and hid. Shaking, terrified, he cried for a long time, holding his hand over the cut on his jaw.

Two hours later, he walked into the cabin that was his home here in this Gold Rush mining camp. He averted his eyes from a certain building that was within view: a small building of heavy logs, with no windows. This was the makeshift jail in Skinner's Hill, and currently the lodging of one Tipton Barth, the brother of Leroy Barth. He was a man accused of the murder of another miner in a claim dispute . . . a knifing murder Micah had witnessed, and which had haunted his dreams ever since.

Micah's mother, one of the relatively few women living in Skinner's Hill mining camp—a community that had sprung to life a year before and that would probably die as quickly once its streams and gullies had yielded up all their gold—saw the cut on his face at once. He'd hoped she'd not notice.

"Whoa, there, young man . . . let me see that face of yours."

Micah stopped and let her examine him. He could not, for some reason, let his gaze meet hers.

She looked at the cut with concern. "This looks like a knife cut, Micah."

"No, Mama," he said, trying to sound convincing and firm. "I scraped it on a nail."

"That doesn't look like a scrape, son. How would you get a scrape in that shape?"

"I'm not a liar, Mama!"

She pulled back, surprised at his forcefulness. Micah blinked and looked away from her.

"All right, son. Whatever you say."

He went up to his loft room and lay down on

his bed. This was something not generally allowable in the hardworking Ward household during daylight hours, but he felt the need for the childish comfort of his sleeping place. He dug deeply beneath the covers and hoped he wouldn't cry again.

"Micah, are you in bed up there?"

"Yes, Mama."

"It's not even suppertime yet!"

"I'm feeling sick, Mama."

She came up the loft ladder after him and laid her hand across his forehead. "You don't feel hot."

"I'm sick. I'm not lying to you."

She looked at him in silent concern. Her eyes traced the line of the cut along his jaw. "I believe you, son," she said. "You rest until I call in your father for supper."

Chapter Two

Micah truly was feeling sick. His terror was deep, indescribable. He couldn't shake from his mind the horrible imagined vision of Leroy Barth cutting out his eyes.

He envisioned his face with dead eyes like Barth's own right eye. He imagined himself blind beside the graves of his murdered family.

Despite all the gentle but clear admonitions his father had given him, all the somber sermons about duty and courage, he knew he couldn't testify to what he'd seen Tipton Barth do to poor old Jim Sneed. If he did, Leroy Barth would do everything he'd threatened.

Micah ate no supper, did not even descend to

join his parents at the table. His appetite was gone. He lay in his loft and listened to his parents eating and talking softly below, in the cabin. His father's voice sounded tired, as always after a long day of mining.

After supper, Joseph Barth climbed to the loft to talk to his son. He sat on the edge of Micah's bed, a sturdy bed whose frame Joe had built himself from straight sapling logs and whose mattress he had stuffed by hand.

"Your mama tells me you got a scrape on your face today, Micah."

Micah briefly let him see the cut.

"Well, could have been worse," Joe Ward said. "It's a peculiar cut to have been made by a nail. Two cuts, really. We'll keep a watch on it to make sure it don't fester. You're feeling kind of sick now?"

"Yes."

Joe nodded. After a brief silence, he said, "Wouldn't be worrying about having to testify against Tipton Barth, would you?"

Micah couldn't answer.

Joe went on: "Because if you are, it'd be an expected thing. It's hard to do the right thing sometimes. But still we got to do it. That's the way the good Lord wrote the rules, you know."

Micah hoped he wouldn't start crying again.

"All you got to do, son, is sit in that chair and tell the truth. We've got us no real nor official court up here, just a miner's court, but we want it to be a fair one. It's to the honor of the men of Skinner's Hill that they've chose to have a real trial, not just a vigilante hanging. You understand the difference between vigilance committees and real courts?"

Micah nodded. He understood it well, from hearing his father's impassioned pleas with the other miners of this community to deal with the murder of Jim Sneed in as close to an orderly, law-abiding, systematic manner as could be achieved in a remote mining camp.

They'd agreed with Joseph Ward in the end and appointed a judge, a prosecutor, and defense attorney, and even a rotating squad of jailers to keep watch over Tipton Barth in his makeshift jail.

The prosecutor and defense attorney were real lawyers, one from Ohio, the other from Georgia. Attorneys were not hard to find in mining camps, where legal wranglings over mining claims and the like made their services valuable.

"That we're prosecuting Tipton Barth in a legal style makes it all the more important that nothing but the pure truth be told," Joe gently lectured. "That places a burden on your shoulders, son, for you are the only witness to the crime. And I know it's probably a heavy burden on your shoulders. Am I right?"

Tears welled despite Micah's attempts to stop

them. He nodded quickly. If only his father knew just how heavy that burden was right now!

"I don't want you to worry about anything," Joe said. "Tipton is locked up. He's a mean man, but he can't hurt you. The men here, me most of all, will protect you from him. All that lies ahead for him is a trial, an almost certain conviction, a sentencing, and a hanging." Joe paused somberly at that point. "Maybe I shouldn't have said the last part. I don't want you to worry about what sentence is carried out on Tipton Barth, son. That's not your concern at all, but that of the grown-up men. All your job is is to tell the truth. You understand?"

"Yes, Pap," Micah managed to say.

"Good. Good." Joe patted his son's shoulder. "You want us to bring you up some food?"

Micah still was not hungry, but he nodded anyway.

When the food arrived, he managed to eat a little of it. Then he rolled over in his bed and pretended to go to sleep, but it was in fact a long and mostly sleepless night. When he did sleep, he dreamed that Leroy Barth had hold of him and was poking out his eyes.

Don't worry about Tipton Barth, his father had told him. But what about Leroy? He was in no jail, and he wouldn't hang. And he was an even meaner man than his murdering brother.

* * *

The court met outside. Tables were set up in a clearing, and a desk for the judge. Tipton Barth sat beside his attorney, arms crossed over his chest and a dark, contemptuous glower on his face. He was a big man, not quite as ugly as his brother because he had both his eyes. But he was scarred and rugged, touched by the marks of many past brawls.

Micah tried not to look at him. Glancing around at the encircling crowd, he saw at the rear of it Leroy Barth, staring at him, grinning cruelly. In that brief and unwanted moment when his gaze locked with Leroy's, Barth winked at him, then let the smile fade for half a moment, reminding Micah of what he was expected to do and what would happen if he failed.

The trial began. It was all an unheard, meaningless buzz to Micah, who stared at the ground. He felt an overwhelming sense of unreality, and in a way it was as welcome as it was unpleasant. Best not to go through this with a clear head. Best to experience this as something not quite real, like the nightmare it was.

"Micah?" His father nudged him. "Didn't you hear? It's time for you to testify."

Micah jerked his head up. All eyes were on him.

"Come on, son," the judge said. "We need to hear from you."

"Are you sick, son?" Joe Ward asked. "You look a little pale."

"I'm . . . I don't know." Micah stood. He walked mechanically to his seat. They made him raise his hand, swear to tell the truth, in the name of God. Micah had been taught to take vows seriously, especially those that evoked the name of God, for God was to be feared. But right now he knew that he feared Leroy Barth much more.

Chapter Three

He never fully remembered all that followed. He answered questions, spoke up more loudly when told to, which was frequent, and saw the bewilderment on the faces of most. Only the Barth brothers looked happy.

Joe Ward had nothing to say to him when at last the ordeal was done and he had returned to his seat.

He'd been afraid he might cry and embarrass himself when all this was done. Instead he just felt numb.

Joe Ward climbed to the loft that night and sat down at the edge of Micah's bed. He filled and lit his pipe. Micah lay there looking at his silent father out of the corner of his eye, smelling the pipe smoke. He usually liked the smell, but tonight nothing could give him pleasure.

"Did you tell the truth today, Micah?" Joe asked at last.

"Yes, Pap." Micah felt his lie ring in his own ears.

"You sure? For what you said today, and what you'd said before . . ."

"I told the truth, Pap. I didn't see him kill nobody."

Joe wouldn't look at him. He puffed at the pipe, then nodded. "Very well, then. So you lied to us before."

"I didn't lie."

"You said before that you saw Tipton Barth kill poor old Sneed."

"I thought I had. . . . I was wrong, though. I didn't really see nothing."

Now Joe did look at him. "Did someone get to you, Micah? Threaten you?"

It was hard not to cry. "No, Pap."

Joe nodded again. "A man walked free today who most were sure was a killer. I hope he truly is innocent, for if he's not, an injustice has happened."

Micah felt a weight descend upon him, wrap itself around him, root into him. This burden he would not easily shrug off.

"The Barth brothers have left," Joe said. "They

rode out today, after Tipton was cleared. Thank God they're gone, at least."

"Yes." It was a heartfelt agreement.

"Good night, son. I hope you sleep well."

"Thank you. You too, Pap."

When Joe was gone and crawling into his own bed below, beside his already sleeping wife, Micah buried his face in his covers and wept silently.

Then he slept, the deep and dreamless sleep of the emotionally exhausted, and for a time was free of that crushing burden.

But the burden was there when he awakened. He felt it as he rose, felt it as he ate a breakfast he did not even taste.

Later in the day, he found himself approaching the claim of Flavius Miller, who had come overland from Illinois right after the rush began.

Miller had no partners, working his claim alone. Some found him aloof, but to Micah he had always been kindly. He was a preacher, sometimes conducting worship services on Sunday mornings for those miners who wished to come. The Wards were generally among them.

He stopped working as Micah approached, and greeted him.

"Hello, Micah. How are you today?"

"I'm fine. . . . No. No, I'm not. There's something . . . I have this kind of feeling like a stone between my shoulders, and . . ." Micah trailed off, realizing he was talking nonsense.

Miller looked a little puzzled, but seemed to take him seriously. "Got something on your conscience, son?"

Micah wondered if he knew. Everybody had known about the Barth trial and Micah's role. Everybody had been talking about how what Micah saw would send Barth to the noose. Then Micah had sat down in the witness chair and said he'd seen nothing at all.

"There's . . . I can't . . ." Micah trailed off again, realizing there was really nothing he could say. He had this sense that if he spoke, Leroy Barth would somehow instantly, mystically know. And he'd take his vengeance even now, with his murdering brother freed.

"Let's talk a few minutes," the preacher said.

Somehow, over the next hour, Micah managed to convey to the preacher his overwhelming pain, his sense of guilt, his fear, without expressly admitting what he'd done. If Miller figured out on his own what Micah had done, he didn't speak it.

They talked of many things that Micah had heard in church, about guilt and sin and forgiveness. Micah followed most of it.

When he was through talking, the preacher stepped inside his cabin and returned with a book. He handed it to Micah. It was a leather-bound Bible, the same one Miller held when he'd preach on Sunday mornings.

"I want you to have that," he said. "I've got another one. You take that book, and you read it. What questions you have, you'll find answers for there."

Micah accepted the Bible. "Thank you."

"Son, I don't know just what this burden you carry is, though I suppose I could make guesses. Whatever it is, though, you look in that book for an answer. And don't stop looking until you find it. That book has given me peace for years and years. It can do the same for you."

Micah touched the leather cover, feeling its rough texture.

"You read that book, starting tonight," Miller said. "Will you do that?"

"I will," Micah said.

Chapter Four

Pardueville, Kansas, many years later

Micah Ward raised the Bible above his head and looked out across the congregation.

"And it was just as that mining camp preacher told me it would be," he said, winding down now to the conclusion of his sermon. "In this book, whose covers have nearly worn away from all the years I've pored over it, I found that peace I sought. And it's been my privilege for years now to share that same book and its message with such as you, my people and my dear friends."

He paused and examined the faces of these people he loved. "Three years, three years this very day. That's how long you have given me the pleasure of being among you, being your friend and shepherd. The role of preacher was not one I had grown up believing I would ever hold. But God, as is so often said, moves in mysterious ways. Through tragedy, fear . . . through guilt . . . he builds avenues to reach those whom he will. And he reached me, changed me, and brought me to you. I thank you for the privilege of being your pastor."

He received nods and smiles. Micah's heart warmed. Truly he did love these people, and they loved him in return.

Micah glanced at his wife, Alice, who sat in her usual spot on the second pew. She gave him the smallest and most subtle of winks—her familiar signal that he had spoken well, that his sermon had been what he intended.

That wifely support meant much to him. He was no educated preacher, not formally anyway, and he'd entered the ministry with some trepidation. Did he really have the ability to do the task he believed he was called to do? How could such a man as he, with little schooling and no right to call himself a scholar, preach adequately to a congregation of people looking to him for leadership?

But he'd done it, and so far, it seemed, he was succeeding. Though preaching paid little, and he had to rely on farming to keep himself and Alice fed, he found it fulfilling.

There was not a day that passed that he did not thank God for the day that he'd been handed that Bible in Skinner's Camp. That was the start of it, the thing that set him on the path toward a new kind of life, and the pulpit.

He lifted his hand. "Let's rise now and have our closing prayer. Brother Meadows, if you'd lead us, I'd be very obliged to you."

Micah leaned on the pulpit with his head bowed, listening to the deacon's prayer, but thinking mostly about the sermon he'd just preached. It had been a personally difficult one. In it he'd come as close as he'd ever dared to telling the story of the Barth brothers and his failure to tell the truth in that long-ago murder trial.

He'd prayed for forgiveness for that failure many times, for it had taken him a long time to believe God could ever forgive anyone for letting a murderer walk free. At last, though, peace had come, and he'd been able to put that event behind him.

He now thought seldom about the failure itself, and instead concentrated on the good things it had led to: that visit to Flavius Miller, the gift of the Bible . . . the changing of his life.

He'd come close to telling the full story today, but no more than close. Not even his beloved Alice knew about the trial, the threats by

Tipton Barthth, his lie under oath. He'd not been able to bring himself to tell her, nor could he see anything to gain even if he could. He'd never told a living soul about what had happened.

When the prayer was finished, Micah made his way to the door of the church to shake the hands of his congregation members as they filed out. They complimented his sermon, gave him smiles and thanks, pats on the shoulder. He felt deeply happy.

Of all those who filed past him, only one was a stranger, but even he was someone Micah had seen before. He was a newcomer to Pardueville who'd opened up a wagon-repair business in an old rented barn at the edge of town. Micah had seen him working about the place, and had been told his name was Tower. Beyond that he knew nothing of the man.

"Good preaching, Reverend," Tower said, smiling but somehow not managing to look convincing at it. Micah had noticed before that the man always looked sad.

"Thank you," Micah replied. "And good to have you with us. Mr. Tower, I think? The wagon man?"

"That's me. Jack Tower. Newcomer here."

"Are you a church member anywhere?"

"Belonged to a little Baptist church down in Texas. That's been some years back, though. I've moved around since then. . . . The truth is, I sort of let church and such get away from me for a few years."

"Well, that happens sometimes. The important thing is, you've come back. I'm glad you chose to be here." Micah paused, curious about the man—for visitors to the church were relatively rare—but not sure how much he should ask. Western folks usually didn't take well to too much prying.

Micah decided to take a chance. "Have you got family, Mr. Tower?"

It was as if he'd just jabbed the man with a long needle. Tower actually winced a little, and it seemed to Micah that his eyes moistened almost instantly.

"No," Tower said tightly. "No family." He turned away. "Good day, preacher."

Micah watched him walk away, heading for a buggy parked at the edge of the churchyard. Tower climbed into the buggy and drove away.

Chapter Five

Alice came to her husband and gave him a kiss on the cheek. Except for their son, they were alone now.

"Wonderful sermon, Micah."

"Thank you . . . but I think I just made a wrong move."

"What?"

He told her about the brief meeting with Tower, and the fact he'd obviously stung him with his intrusive question. "I'm afraid he might not come back," Micah said. "I shouldn't have been so inquisitive."

"It's hard to know how people will react to questions," Alice said. "If it concerns you, maybe you can go visit him and make amends. Isn't he the man who works on wagons over in town?"

"Yes." He watched as Tower's buggy disappeared over the low rise, dust boiling out behind it. It had been a long and dry autumn. "Maybe I will."

"Micah . . . your sermon today . . ." She trailed off, as if hesitant to speak further.

He looked at her. "I thought you liked my sermon."

"I did like it," she said. "But you talked about things that make me . . . curious, I guess."

She'd said things like this before, when he'd drifted close in conversation or sermons to the Barth incident.

"You want to know what happened to me when I was a boy," he said.

"Yes. I admit that I do, Micah. Whatever it was, obviously it was something that terrified you and made you feel guilty. You're the man I love, so it's only natural I want to know."

"I understand. But it's not something I want to tell, dear. There's nothing gained by it. All you need to know is that it happened, that by the grace of God I made it through, and the entire thing led me to a mining camp preacher and the beginning of a new life." He smiled at her. "So don't worry, and don't let this curiosity eat you up."

"Just tell me this: Were you hurt?"

For a moment he felt the sting of that knife again, and his face gave the smallest of twitches. He fought back the impulse to touch the faint, T-shaped scar that still marked his face where Leroy Barth had cut him. His smile, though, remained. "No, not in any kind of significant or lasting way," he answered.

She wasn't satisfied, and he could tell it, but she made the best of it. "I suppose I'll have to just let it go, then. But maybe, Micah, someday . . . maybe you'll tell me?"

"Maybe." But in fact he had no intention ever of doing so.

"Are you hungry?" she asked.

"Starved."

"The stew is ready," she said. "As soon as the corn bread bakes, we'll eat." She looked around. "Where's Flavius gotten to?" Flavius was their son, named by Micah after Flavius Miller, who'd given him the Bible and changed his life.

"Out running with his dog, I think," Micah said. "I'll go find him.

Micah finished his last bite of corn bread and pushed his plate away. He chewed slowly, deep in thought.

"What's on your mind, dear?" Alice asked.

"Hmm? Oh . . . just thinking about Jack Tower. Our church visitor. I think I'll give him some business."

"The buckboard wheel?" Alice said in a hopeful tone. The vehicle had been an inheritance of Alice's, left to her by an uncle who died without children, and she had always been proud of it because it was a fairly luxurious item, the sort she and Micah would never buy on their own. But the right wheel had recently been squeaking and wobbly to the extent Micah had been afraid for her to use the buckboard.

"That's right. It needs repair anyway, and it would be a chance for me to get to know him a little. Maybe persuade him to come back and visit church again."

"I found a dead snake in the woods," Flavius announced in the abrupt manner of little boys.

"Oh, honey, don't tell us about it while we're eating."

Flavius shrugged and went back to his stew.

"Jack Tower carries heavy burdens," Alice said.

"How can you know that?" Micah asked.

"Can't you tell?" Alice said. "You can see a sorrow in him that is very deep indeed."

"If so, maybe I can be a source of help to him," Micah replied. "Flavius, send that corn bread this way."

"Mick Branchfield is going to fight Jimmy," Flavius declared in another sudden change of subject.

"How do you know?"

"He was saying so at church."

"And I'll bet you weren't supposed to tell it, either," Micah said.

"Why, Micah, he ought to tell such things when he knows them," Alice remonstrated. "Boys don't need to be fighting each other."

Micah scooped a chunk of potato out of his stew and watched the steam rise from it. "No," he said. "They shouldn't. But you ought not tell things you hear in confidence, either."

"Oh, it wasn't in confidence," Flavius said sincerely. "He ain't confident about it at all."

Micah and his wife glanced at each other with little smiles.

"Not confident, huh?" Micah said. "Then why is he planning to fight?"

"He says he's got to. Jimmy won't leave him alone. He's been picking on him for nearly the whole year, and Mick's been trying to stay away from him, and that ain't working. So he says he's got to quit running away from it and face up to it."

"That sounds like Mick," Alice said. "When he talks, it's like hearing a grown-up talk. You ever noticed that about him, Micah?"

"I have. I've also noticed that he's about half the size of Jimmy. He's likely to get whupped."

"Mick knows that," Flavius said. "But he says he's got to show Jimmy he ain't afraid of him and that he won't run from him no more."

"Well, I admire his courage, anyway," Micah said. "Even though I can't condone fighting. The Bible tells us to turn the other cheek, and to bless those who try to hurt us."

"What about that time Jesus ran them bank tellers out of the church house with that great big bullwhip?" Flavius asked.

"It was a temple, not a church, and I don't believe he had a bullwhip," Micah said. "I don't know that they had bullwhips back then. And they weren't bank tellers. They were money changers."

"Yeah, but what I mean is, sometimes there's times you got to just deal with things, ain't there? Without being nice about it?"

"I don't think you can draw a comparison between Jesus running the money changers out of the temple and Jimmy and Mick getting into a fight."

"I think you should tell Mick's parents he's planning to fight," Alice said to her son.

Micah spoke up. "Now, honey, he can't do that. Boys don't go tattling. It's kind of against the rules of being a boy." He winked at Flavius, who grinned back.

"Even if somebody can get hurt?"

"They're just two boys, Alice. They won't hurt each other."

Alice sighed and shook her head. "I swear, I

don't understand men sometimes. Or boys. The way you think, and act . . ."

"It's not hard, Ma," Flavius said. "It's just that, sometimes, a man or a boy just has to fight. 'Cause there ain't no other way. Right, Pa?"

"Right, son. Not often. But sometimes."

Chapter Six

The sky was cloudy, the wind kicking up, the temperature dropping, and the buckboard wheel squeaking and wobbling worse than ever the next morning when Micah drove it into town. He'd come alone and was glad of it, because he feared the wheel might break or simply fall off at almost any moment, and he never liked to go through such little disasters with Alice around. She tended to get overly worried about such things.

There wasn't much to Pardueville. It was a perfectly flat little community, laid out in a neat grid pattern because there were no intruding features of the landscape to create a need for any street to curve and break up the checkerboard pattern.

Jack Tower's wagon-repair business operated in what had been a barn at the south edge of town. Tower had done little to make the barn look like a place of business. He'd not even put up a sign. Only the various wagons parked around the front of it, in various states of repair, and the wagon wheels leaned against the barn wall, made the current use of the place evident.

Tower wasn't to be seen as Micah drove the wagon into the lot. The barn door was open. Micah figured he was inside.

"Hello!" he said loudly as he pulled the creaking buckboard to a halt. "Anybody around?"

He heard what he thought was a reply from somewhere inside the barn. Tower's voice. But it had a harsh edge, and then a second voice spoke, more loudly, also harsh.

"Hello?" Micah said again, climbing down from the buckboard and heading for the door.

He heard Tower's voice again. "I told you I didn't think it would hold! I warned you that it would give way. But you insisted I not replace it."

"An axle should last longer than a week, and you know it!" the other voice replied, nearly shouting.

Micah recognized the speaker and winced. Henry Pierce, another local farmer, renowned for his sour disposition, short temper, and tightfistedness. Micah had never liked to be around him, and felt guilty for his own secret gladness that Pierce was not part of his congregation.

"A new axle would have lasted as long as the wagon itself," Tower replied. "But you wouldn't let me give you a new axle. That's the whole damn point!"

Micah stopped at the edge of the door, frowning, sorry to hear Tower's swearing.

"This is a damn wagon-repair shop, ain't it?" Pierce shot back. "If I'd wanted a new axle, I could just buy myself a new wagon right along with it! I wanted my old axle fixed!"

"And fixed it was."

"It ain't fixed if it breaks within the week!"

"I told you, damn it all, that it wouldn't hold! And you wouldn't the hell listen!" Tower's voice had risen even more all at once, taking on a new, threatening quality. Micah actually backed away from the door a couple of steps. "Now, get your damned and sorry old hide out of this shop! Now! Before I break your neck like that axle!"

There was a brief pause, then Pierce said, "What are you doing with that? You put that hammer down!"

"I'll sink it in your worthless skull, you damned old fool!" Tower yelled back at him. "Get out! Get out of here, now!"

"I ought to have the law on you, threatening me like that!"

"Out! And don't come back here, you mealy-mouthed old devil!"

Micah heard Pierce storm out the back door of the barn. A moment later he saw him circle back around through the side lot and head for the street, walking in a fast, angry stride. Pierce looked back toward the barn, and Micah noticed that his face was pale. The man was scared.

Pierce saw Micah standing there and paused. "There's your churchgoing types for you, preacher!" Pierce called back. "Did you hear what he just said to me?"

Without awaiting an answer, Pierce turned again and stalked on up the street.

Micah decided to leave without making his presence known to Jack Tower. This obviously was not a good time to make a call.

But just as he turned back toward the buck-board, Tower appeared at the door. He froze for a moment when he saw the preacher there, and his red, angry-looking face lost a little of its color.

Micah and Tower looked silently at each other a moment.

"Hello, Mr. Tower," Micah said.

"Preacher," Tower replied, barely audible.

Micah nodded, uncomfortable, tried to find something to say, and couldn't. He nodded again and headed back to the buckboard.

Climbing aboard, he drove off with the wheel

wobbling and squeaking, and did not look back at Jack Tower.

The sunset was a brilliant red. Micah, pausing from his labors with hammer in hand, studied it and give a quiet prayer of thanks for its beauty. Such sights exhilarated him.

This evening, though, he didn't respond quite as powerfully as usual. He'd been depressed ever since returning from Tower's wagon shop this morning, the buckboard still unrepaired.

Micah was not naive. He knew that, as a preacher, he generally saw people on their best behavior. Most folks grew quite righteous when he came into their presence, and he was quite certain that much of that righteousness faded as soon as he was gone.

Still, to hear Tower cursing and lambasting that unhappy customer had been unusually troubling. He'd assumed that, since Tower had visited his church, he was a different sort than that.

He chuckled at himself. Maybe he was naive after all. Hadn't Tower himself told him he'd drifted away from the church for years? Why should he assume the man would be some sort of saint just because he darkened a church door occasionally?

Micah lowered his gaze from the sky and saw a rider approaching from the direction of town. Micah squinted, trying to make out who it was.

He heard the side door of his house open and Alice call him and Flavius in for supper. Flavius, who had been playing with his dog in the yard, hopped up and ran toward the house, but Micah called back, "I'll be in in a minute, dear."

He'd just made out who was approaching.

Jack Tower rode to the gate and stopped there.

Micah approached him, dusting sawdust and grit off his hands.

"Mr. Tower, sir. Welcome to my house."

"Hello, preacher." He looked around. "Nice place."

"Thank you. It's small but sufficient. There's only the three of us here. Please, dismount and come over to the porch."

"I may have come at a time to interrupt your supper."

"Interrupt? No, no. In fact, join us."

"I couldn't do that."

"Sure you can. I insist. Alice always has more than enough food fixed."

"Obliged. And then, after . . . maybe you and me can talk in private a bit."

Micah had seen that one coming. As soon as he'd recognized Tower, he'd figured the man was coming to apologize to him for his behavior with that customer earlier in the day.

Alice was surprised but welcoming when Micah appeared inside with the unanticipated guest. She quickly laid out another plate and took Tower's hat and coat. Flavius, always glad for visitors, immediately began chattering at Tower, giving the man little chance to respond but also relaxing him, making him feel welcome.

The Wards and their guest ate slowly, talking about unimportant things. Alice apologized for the lack of a dessert, but Tower waved it off.

"The meal itself was dessert enough for me," he said. "I live alone, you see, and what I fix for myself ain't much worth having most of the time."

"Do you enjoy cigars?" Micah asked.

"I do."

"Then we'll make that our dessert. I've got a box of good ones, all the way from Chicago."

"So you're not a preacher who minds the use of tobacco."

"I enjoy a cigar every now and again," Micah replied. "I think the key is moderation. Let's step outside and enjoy a couple . . . moderately, of course."

Chapter Seven

Out on the porch, with cigars nicely lit and flaring red-tipped in the darkness, Micah had to send Flavius back inside to allow Tower the opportunity to talk in private.

"You can probably guess why I came," he said, scratching the back of his neck uncomfortably.

"My guess is that you want to apologize to me for having cursed and acted as you did with that customer today."

"Yes. I didn't know you were there. I'd have controlled myself better if I had. Or I think I would have."

"There's no need to apologize to me, Mr. Tower. If you feel you acted in the wrong way, then apologize to the Lord, and to the man you were speaking to."

"But you being a preacher and all . . ."

"I'll be forthright with you, Mr. Tower. One thing that sometimes can irritate preachers is the tendency of people to become all false and tense whenever the local clergyman comes around. As I said, if you think you did wrong today, apologize to the ones you think you may have insulted, not to me."

"I will apologize. Although that fellow today ought to apologize to me as well. He was quite belligerent. He insulted my work, and I don't abide that very easily."

"You men of business have to put up with a lot of nonsense from the public, no doubt about it."

"Indeed. It could try the patience of Job sometimes. There's days I wish I could just disappear."

They puffed on their cigars for a time, silent. Then Tower cleared his throat and spoke again.

"I'd like to tell you something, Preacher. Just so you'll know more about me and why maybe I sometimes don't act as I should, like I did today. What you saw there this morning wasn't my usual nature. Only over the last year or so have I tended to lose my temper that way."

"Why's that?"

"Because of what happened . . . to my family."

"I see. Something bad, I gather."

"They were taken from me, suddenly." He held a brief silence. "Murdered."

"Murdered!"

"Yes, sir. My wife's name was Angeline. My baby boy was Bradley, and my daughter was Nancy."

"You're telling me that all three of them were killed?"

"Yes. Back in Colorado, where we lived. I came to Kansas fleeing the memories of it all. But I think they've followed me."

"I'm shocked, Mr. Tower. And horrified. What a terrible thing! I don't know what to say."

"There's no words that can help, really. It was worse than a straight-out murder, Preacher. My wife was . . . misused. My little Nancy, thank God, they left alone in that way, her being so young. But she fought them on behalf of her mother, and they struck her with a pistol butt and killed her."

Micah stared at his cigar, having suddenly lost all taste for it. He watched the coal slowly go dark as Tower continued.

"I was gone at the time it happened. Away on business. Nobody knows exactly what happened. The best guess is that the pair of them came to my house and gained entrance on some pretext or the other. Angeline was always ready to feed a stranger or lend a hand. A fine woman she was. Your own wife's manner reminds me of her. Anyway, they got in, and took advantage. When they'd killed them, they stole every kind of little thing of value they could from the house, Angeline's wedding ring and jewelry her mother had given her and such. They set the house afire and left. The blaze went out, though. But not until it had smoked up the house so bad that my little baby boy, upstairs in his crib, died from smothering in it. Angeline and Nancy were already dead downstairs, Nancy from the blow to the head, Angeline from strangling."

Micah let the dead cigar fall from his fingers to the porch. "I'm sickened, Mr. Tower. And amazed you can even bring yourself to recount this to me so . . . dispassionately."

"You grow accustomed to it. Not accepting of it, not peaceful about it . . . just accustomed to the facts of what happened. There's nothing I can do to change it. And I wanted you to know why I might seem an odd man at times, Preacher. And not consistent. My emotions and such, you see, the state of my mind . . . it's all different because of the killing."

"I can understand that."

"I want to ask you, Preacher, not to share what we're talking about here. Not even with your wife. It's something I feel compelled to keep to myself. You're the first person here I've told."

"I'll say nothing." It would be hard to resist

sharing such startling knowledge with Alice, but he'd keep his promise.

"Did they catch the killers?" Micah asked.

"A posse caught up with one of them. He fought back and they shot him dead on the spot. The other got away."

"Do you think he'll be caught?"

"I don't know. He should have been caught years before. That pair has killed others, you see. Many people over the years, from what I hear. All across the West."

"I don't know what to say to you about all this, Mr. Tower."

"Call me Jack. And there's nothing for you to say. What is, is. I just wanted you to know about it. I ain't making excuses for misbehaviors. Just giving explanation. Before I lost my family, I wouldn't so much as whisper a cussword or yell at nobody. But now, sometimes, I grow like I was earlier today. I let out rage at folks who don't deserve it." He hesitated, then added, "Sometimes I even say blasphemous things to God. I want to curse him for having let my family be so mistreated. I curse myself for not having been there to keep my family safe. And I curse all the people who might have stopped the murderers before they ever got to my house and my family. They say that there'd been many times before that this pair had gotten away with crimes. They'd intimidate people away from testifying against them and so on. Or so they tell me."

That struck a little too close to home for Micah. He fidgeted and stood, pacing a little.

Tower took it as a sign he should move on, and stood as well.

"Thank you, Preacher Ward. I appreciate you listening to me. And I pledge to you and to the Lord that I'll try to keep my temper better in the future, and watch my language."

Micah said, "That seems a small thing now, knowing what you've suffered."

"There's those who have suffered more than me. And those who have suffered since me. The killer who got away has murdered two others, you see. One a town marshal, the other a fellow he murdered just to get his horse. I wish he could have been killed along with his brother."

"It was two brothers?" Micah asked.

"Yes. At least the one-eyed one is gone now. Well, good night. Thank your wife again for the victuals."

Tower turned and headed for his horse, which was still tethered at the gate.

"Jack . . ."

He turned. "Yes?"

"These brothers . . . what did you say their name was?"

"I didn't say. But it's Barth. Tipton and Leroy.

Leroy was the one killed by the posse. Good night again."

Micah tried to reply, but his voice was gone. He could hardly breathe.

He managed to remain standing until Jack Tower had mounted up and ridden away some distance, and then his knees buckled and he sank to the porch, limp and weak and feeling he might become sick on the spot.

Chapter Eight

Long past midnight, Alice Ward rolled over in her bed and sat up.

Micah was out of bed, sitting in a chair by the window, staring out.

"Micah? Why are you up?"

"Couldn't sleep."

"Is something wrong?"

He did not answer.

"Micah? Are you sick? You looked pale after you came back in."

"So you already told me. No, I'm not sick."

"Come back to bed, Micah?"

"Later."

"But you need your rest."

"Later."

She knew better than to ask again. She watched his dark form there in the dark room, vaguely silhouetted against the window, and felt a deep, unsettling concern. She lay back down and waited for him to come to bed. He did not, and eventually she drifted off to sleep again.

When she awakened in the morning, Micah was in bed beside her, sleeping, but he woke up as she slipped out of bed, and a few minutes later got out of bed himself.

He said hardly a handful of words all day. Alice didn't see him smile even once.

Two days later, Alice was in the kitchen, cutting up chicken for the night's supper and staring at the wall, thinking hard and feeling very troubled.

The door opened and Flavius came in, head turned away to hide his face. He passed by her quickly and entered the next room, but as he did so, she saw him lift a hand and dab at his eye.

"Flavius?" she asked. "Is something wrong?"

He mumbled something back at her.

She wiped her hands clean and went after him. He was sitting in a chair, looking upset, and quickly turned his head away when she came in.

"Flavius, you're crying."

"I'm not."

"Come on, son. Tell me what's happened."

"It's Pap. He yelled at me. I was trying to help

him, and I dropped the lumber. It was an accident, but he yelled at me."

"I'm sure he didn't mean to."

"He did. He was mad. He's been mad for days."

Alice sighed, walked over, and knelt beside Flavius's chair. "I don't think he's mad, exactly. He's just got something on his mind."

"Something I did?"

"No. I don't think it has anything to do with you. The truth is I don't know what it is."

"It started after Mr. Tower came and ate supper with us."

Alice thought about it, and realized Flavius was right. She hadn't made the connection until then.

"Flavius, did you hear any of what they talked about on the porch?"

"No. Pap sent me away before that."

She frowned, silent. "Well," she said, "I'm sure everything will be all right. And I'm sure your father didn't mean to hurt your feelings."

"I'm worried about things, Mama. Something doesn't seem right."

"Everything is fine, son."

But she wasn't sure it really was.

The wind was up on Saturday evening, whipping across the Kansas plains, twisting into dust devils and slapping the side of the house like a great hand.

Alice looked out the kitchen window. The sunset tonight was even redder than that brilliant one earlier in the week. Almost a bloody red.

She wondered where Micah was. He tended to be hard to find on Saturday evenings, usually off by himself studying for his sermon the next morning.

Alice went looking. He wasn't in the pantry or in his chair up by the bedroom window, two of his usual study retreats. She went to the porch and saw them there, sitting on the edge of the porch with his back turned toward her.

"Studying hard, Micah?" she asked, approaching.

He didn't answer. He was busy with something, and she was shocked to see that he was cleaning his pistol. It was a good pistol, a gift from her own father, who declared that any man west of the Mississippi was doing himself a disservice if he didn't own a good Colt revolver. Micah had always liked the pistol as an ornament and possession, but generally ignored it, not being a man drawn to instruments of violence.

"I haven't seen you clean that pistol in months," she said, sitting down beside him on the porch's edge.

"That's why it needs cleaning," he said.

"I didn't know you'd fired it recently."

"I haven't. I fired it last maybe six months ago. I failed to clean it afterward."

"Are you planning to shoot it again soon?"

"A man should keep in practice with a pistol. He never knows when he might be called upon to use it. Bad things happen. Did you know that there've been families murdered by people who just stop by, asking for a meal or a drink of water?"

"What in the world has put such thoughts into your mind? You're the one who always says that our protection comes from God."

"Things happen, Alice. You can't be naive. You can't be complacent. You can't just sit and expect everything to be fine, for all the bad in the world just to fade away on its own."

"Micah, this doesn't sound like you. Why are you talking so sharply to me?"

"I'm not talking sharply." He rubbed on the pistol with a soft cloth, holding it up. The gleaming metal reflected the bloodred sunset.

"Micah, something's wrong. You've not been yourself ever since Mr. Tower visited here."

"Not myself? Who else am I, then?"

"I don't know. A stranger."

He laughed without humor and shook his head, as if she'd just said something foolish.

"Don't mock me, Micah. This isn't like you."

He looked at her, brows lowered.

"Micah, your eyes are red."

"If you're implying that I've been sitting out

here crying, you're wrong. The wind is in my eyes, that's all."

"But there is something wrong."

"I've had something to think about lately."

"You can't tell me?"

He shook his head.

"When you're ready, Micah."

"Alice, I may have to go somewhere soon. Away."

"Where? Why?"

"Maybe to Colorado. I think I may have to deal with something. Correct a mistake I made once, a long time ago."

She held back the flood of questions that arose. She could not hold back her tears.

"I'm sorry," he said. "I wish I could tell you more."

"Does it have to do with Jack Tower?"

"No. Not really. Not directly."

She would press no further. Forcing a smile, she said, "What will you preach about tomorrow?"

"I don't know," he said. "So far I've not been able to decide."

Chapter Nine

Micah advanced to the pulpit slowly, clutching hard his beloved Bible. He'd sat silently through the hymns and prayers, hearing nothing. At the moment he felt that, somehow, he wasn't really, fully here.

He leaned on the pulpit and looked across the little congregation. Jack Tower was not present, and Micah was grateful. His presence would have only made this harder.

Micah cleared his throat, then said, "I must tell you, right now, that I have nothing to say to you today."

He paused while the congregation members glanced at one another. Alice looked back at him in open puzzlement. Flavius, as usual, had found something to distract him, and seemed to hear nothing as he played about with a little stick he'd picked up on the way in.

Micah went on. "There are times when a preacher of the gospel can feel God speaking through him, flowing through him like water in a streambed. There are times when the flow dries up. This is one of those times."

He held up his Bible. "In this book I've found the answers for my life. Now I find that it seems closed to me. I've read, I've prayed, I've meditated, and prayed some more. And it seems clear to me that there's something I must do. Until it's done, there will be no more answers for me. And therefore, I'm telling you that as of today, I'm stepping down as your pastor."

He paused again, letting the realization sink in. Now even Flavius was paying attention.

"It's my hope that you will let me return later. It will be weeks at the least, maybe months. There's a task I must perform. Something I have to set straight."

Several people were looking at Alice, as if to receive an explanation from her, but she had none to give. Her expression grew stony and she gazed straight ahead, looking at no one, including her husband.

"I ask only one thing of you, and that is for your prayers," Micah said. "I don't know whether what I'm setting out to do is what God would have me do. . . . I hope it is, but I don't know. And how I'll deal with the situation I may encounter . . . I don't know that, either." He looked around at the confused faces. "I know this is difficult to understand. I know that you may not wish to have me remain your pastor when this is through. If not, I will understand. Maybe, by that point, I'll understand a lot more about many things than I do now."

Alice was fighting hard to maintain her statue-like expression. And Flavius, confused, was on the verge of crying.

"There's no sermon today," Micah said. "Well, maybe there is, if only a brief one. It's this: Don't think the ghosts of your past will go away. They don't. They may hide for years, but they come back. And they call you to come face them. And now, that's what I've got to do. So, for now, good-bye, and amen. And while I'm gone, take care of my family for me. Thank you."

The people rose and crowded in on him as he left the pulpit, but he answered no questions. Alice stayed in her pew, and Flavius came to her side and wrapped his arms around her, clinging and looking at his father as if he'd become a stranger.

Micah went to them. "I'm sorry," he said. "Later, maybe, I can tell you more."

Alice looked away, and Flavius clutched her all the harder.

Flavius winced with the boom of each shot. He was in the house, with his mother, looking out the window, watching his father in a field about a quarter of a mile away.

Micah was firing the pistol, aiming at a tree. He would fire until the pistol was empty, reload, and fire it empty again.

"Why is Pap practicing his shooting?" Flavius asked. "He never liked shooting before."

"I don't know," Alice replied.

"And why does he have to go away?"

"I don't know that either," she said.

"Will Pap tell us?"

"I don't think so. Not right away. Just pray for him, Flavius. Pray for him very hard."

Micah had owned the horse for three years, and knew it to be skittish about entering enclosed spaces. The railroad crew had to fight hard to cajole the reluctant animal into the railroad car.

Alice had almost not come with him, but had relented at last. She'd clung to him, begging him not to go.

"I have to go," he said. "There's something I should have done years ago, and didn't, that I have to find a way to do now. If I can."

It was Flavius who broke Micah's heart. The

boy comprehended this even less than his mother, and wrapped his arms around Micah like he feared he'd never see him again. He pleaded with Micah to explain why he was going.

But Micah could not explain to another what he could barely understand himself.

Micah knew it would be best not to look at his wife and son as the train pulled out, but of course he had to look. They stood on the station platform, expressions sad and, maybe, in Alice's case, also angry.

He waved at them, trying to make himself smile through the dirty window, and only vaguely succeeding. He didn't feel like smiling. He wanted to weep aloud.

She was angry. It was easy to see. And he couldn't blame her. What sense did any of this make? How he could expect them to understand his behavior when he himself couldn't?

He didn't know why he was doing this . . . didn't even know exactly what he was doing. All he knew was that he had to go to Colorado and try to find a phantom from his past named Tipton Barth.

And then . . .

There's where it grew murky. What would he do if he did find Barth? Preach to him? Say a prayer with him? Give him a Bible?

Kill him?

It was a possibility. God help him, it was indeed a possibility.

There were those, he'd always heard, who would not choose the right. Would not be changed. Would not be converted. Those were the ones, he'd been taught, for whom even God could do nothing except leave them to the consequences of their own actions.

Surely Tipton Barth was one of these. He'd lived his entire life as a killer. He'd never faced the consequences of it. Why would he ever turn away from it?

For the thousandth time in the course of a few days, Micah said mentally to himself: I should have stopped him long ago. It was given to me to see him brought to justice, and I failed, out of fear. A boy's fear. Now I'm a man, and I must not be afraid.

He was afraid, though. Terrified. He knew nothing of manhunting, of capturing murderers, maybe even killing them, if it came to that.

He watched the train station fall out of sight behind him on the Kansas flatlands, then bowed his head and said a prayer for his wife and son.

Micah opened his red carpetbag, pulled out his Bible, and tried to read, but the rocking train made him feel woozy. At last he closed the book and leaned back, staring at the ceiling of the passenger car and wondering what would happen next.

Chapter Ten

The travel seemed endless, but the farther he got from his home, the more Micah relaxed. He'd not expected this, for the travel only brought him closer to Colorado and the manhunt for Tipton Barth. But the truth was that the farther this thing progressed, the more unrealistic it seemed. How likely was it he would find Barth? If the man was a murderer, he was probably not one to stay in one area long.

Micah had spoken to Jack Tower one time since Tower's visit to his property, and found out exactly where Tower had lived while in Colorado. He'd done this in a way to arouse no suspicion on Tower's part, not wanting Tower to know what he had in mind.

Now it all seemed a little ridiculous. He'd reach the town of Greentree and discover that Tipton Barth was long gone. He'd ask a few questions, go through the motions of trying to find the man, and return home with his conscience appeased. Then he could forget about Tipton Barth and events long past and get on with his life.

This whole thing really was foolish. He'd apologize to Alice when he got home, and never do anything like this again.

Another passenger walked past, and inadvertently kicked something out of the aisleway toward Micah. It was a discarded newspaper. Micah leaned over and picked it up.

When he unfolded it and saw the name, he curled his lip in vague contempt. This was a copy of the *American Crime Chronicle,* a rather sordid newspaper headquartered in Denver and published in a unique fashion across the nation. Correspondents across the country would gather and telegraph in to Denver lurid, usually exaggerated stories of murders, robberies, kidnappings, rapes. The stories would be transcribed, quickly illustrated from a standing and ever-growing body of ready-made crime art created and constantly replenished by a pool of artists, and published in first edition out of Denver.

Simultaneously, however, the stories would also be wired in turn to various other key locales across the country, where other versions of the same edition, slightly retooled depending on region, would be published and distributed over the course of about a month. By the time the cycle was complete, it would be time for yet another edition, and it all would repeat.

Micah had little use for the *Chronicle*, and had gone so far as to urge his congregation to shun it. He'd caught Flavius with an old copy or two before, gazing at the sensational illustrations, many of which featured women with exposed limbs, low-cut dresses, and so on.

Micah glanced over the copy of the newspaper, shaking his head. He tossed it aside. Any reading he'd do would be confined to his Bible.

By the time they reached the foot of the Rockies, Micah was extraordinarily weary of train travel. But the weather had grown much colder and snow fell, blanketing the landscape and making it even more wildly beautiful than usual. Micah lost himself in the splendor and sang hymns beneath his breath.

So far his fellow travelers had mostly left him alone, which suited him. What would he say if someone asked him why he was traveling into Colorado? Oh, I'm just trying to find a murderer whom I allowed to go unpunished many years ago, leaving him free to kill and kill again. Once I do find him, I'll either convert him or shoot him dead. . . .

He wondered if he should simply turn around when he reached Greentree and ride back home again right away.

The train reached a steeper grade and curved up the side of a shining mountain. The wind whipped the snow into sharply slanting lines and made the black smoke from the locomotive dance and swirl in the snowy atmosphere. The mountains seemed vast, intimidating.

Micah was pleased when the train reached a more level area and began to slow for a refueling stop. He was nearly starved. By the time the train screeched to a halt at the train station of a little town whose name Micah did not know, he was already heading down the aisle toward the door.

There was no real café in the town, but a woman with a basket was selling sandwiches at the train station. Micah bought two of them and found a seat at the end of a bench on the platform. He positioned himself to avoid the worst of the wind.

He was startled by the sound of a loud collective whoop and burst of raucous laughter. Something small and bright flashed by his feet and launched itself over the edge of the station platform.

What remained of Micah's sandwich fell from his hand as he realized that what he'd just seen was a flaming rat.

He stood, puzzled and horrified. To his right a band of men appeared, five or six of them, all of them noticeably drunk, laughing and slapping one another's shoulders.

"That was a fast one, sure 'nough!" one of them said. "Never seen one run so fast!"

"There he is, down under the platform," another one declared, stooping and pointing. "See him burning? He ain't running now!"

They all seemed to find that funny, and made an absurd show of bending and stooping to see the dying rat. All were so drunk that they could hardly keep their balance, and stumbled about into each other.

Micah was appalled, partly at the drunkenness but mostly at the cruelty. He had no love of rats, but to kill one so viciously made him feel sickened and furious.

Though he wasn't forceful by nature, Micah was about to step forward and confront the group when the approach of another man, equally drunk, distracted them.

The newcomer yelled at the group. "Hey, gents! Got us a dog for this one."

Micah saw a small white dog struggling in the man's arms, and with a sickening feeling realized what was intended for it.

"Where's the coal oil?" one of the drunks bellowed. "Where'd you put the jar, Billy?"

One of the others produced a fruit jar with a clear liquid. Micah had taken it to be homemade whiskey, but now realized it was indeed coal oil.

The man with the dog knelt, holding it, while the one with the jar squatted beside him.

Micah was frozen, unable even to breathe. He looked around. No one else seemed to be aware of what was going on.

Coal oil splashed across the dog, making it yelp and struggle harder. Micah saw one of the men fumbling with a box of matches. . . .

"No!" he shouted, stepping forward. "Let that dog go!"

His shout was so loud that the squatting man with the dog lost his balance and fell back. The dog broke loose and ran away, darting under the train station.

Micah took a deep breath, relieved.

A babble of curses rained at him from the gang of drunks. He hardly noticed. In his mind he imagined the ugly image of that dog, flaming and running. . . . It was intolerable. That such a cruel act would have even been considered by these men as a form of entertainment . . .

One of them was suddenly directly in his face, ranting and shouting, his breath reeking of whiskey.

Micah caught the man's words in midsentence. ". . . your own damned business!" he said. "What the hell you mean, running off my dog!"

Micah stared at the man, silent.

The fellow reached out and shoved him in the chest.

"Keep your hands off me," Micah said.

"You ran off my dog!" the man shouted.

"You were going to set that dog afire, like you did the rat."

"And what the hell's that to you?"

"I don't stand by and let that happen."

"I'm going to beat the hell out of you!" the man yelled. His companions were moving in now, all of them with similar angry expressions. People were certainly taking notice now, and backing away.

Micah realized what a predicament he had placed himself in. He was facing off a group of angry drunks . . . alone.

But when he thought about that dog, and what would have befallen it . . .

"If you want to beat me, go ahead and try," he heard himself say. "I'm not a bit sorry for saving that dog from the kind of cruelty you had planned for it!"

The man shoved Micah again, almost making him fall.

"That's enough," Micah said, and struck the man in the nose with his fist.

He felt bone and cartilage crunch, heard the man suck in his breath in a great gasp, and saw him fall straight back like a felled tree. His drunk companions didn't even try to catch him, but dodged out of the way. He hit the platform with a loud clump.

The drunks stared down at him, then up at Micah, and burst into laughter.

"What are you?" one of them asked. "Some kind of fighter?"

"I'm a preacher," Micah replied, looking down and wondering if he'd killed the man.

"A preacher? A preacher?" The man looked around at his companions. "Horace got knocked out by a preacher!"

They howled with appreciative mirth, gathering around Micah and slapping him on the shoulders. Micah kept looking at the fallen man.

"Is he alive?" he asked.

"Hell, it takes more than that to kill Horace! A preacher! Ain't that a hell of a thing!"

Micah was so bewildered that he grinned for lack of anything else to do.

"Have a drink, preacher!"

"No. No, thank you. I don't touch it."

They treated him like an honored guest until he was back on the train again. He watched through the window as they helped their fallen friend come back around again and make it to his feet. His nose was bloody. But as the train pulled out, the man raised a hand and waved respectfully at Micah.

Micah was more bewildered than ever. He realized that, in a most unexpected way, he'd just gained respect from a breed of man he'd hardly had any dealings with. And he'd gained it in a way he never would have expected.

It grew funny as he thought about it, and he chuckled aloud.

But as the train moved on, he began to think more deeply about what had happened at the train station. He didn't believe in violence. Had he been advising anyone else about how to react to the kind of situation he'd just encountered, he'd have told him to turn the other cheek.

Maybe this time, though, he'd done a better thing by fighting back. He'd not done it intentionally—he'd struck the man purely by reflex—but it had solved a problem.

Maybe the world was a little more complex than he'd thought. Maybe, as the Bible said, there was a time for war as well as a time for peace.

He thought about Tipton Barth, and what might lie ahead.

Lord, he prayed mentally. Whatever may come, if anything, be with me. And if I have to fight again, let me fight well.

Chapter Eleven

Micah was asleep when the crash occurred.

The jolt threw him out of his seat and caused his head to slam against the side of the seat across the aisle. He collapsed into the floor of the passenger car, barely hearing the screams and yells of the other startled travelers.

The car tilted, rolling him, then leveled again, though it rocked like a boat for several moments as if it couldn't decide whether to tilt off the tracks or stay on. He came to rest against the base of another seat. Someone stepped on his arm, then was off him and gone. He groaned and tried to sit up. Someone else ran over him, knocking him back down.

He stayed there a moment until the train stopped rocking. Then he pushed up, groaning again, his head throbbing. He touched it gently, then looked at his fingers. There was blood, but only a little. Just a small abrasion.

The car was in tumult, people moving about, baggage scattering. Micah scooted himself into the space behind a nearby seat, trying to focus his vision and clear his head from the effects of his injury.

At last he rose and headed toward the door. All other passengers by now had already exited.

Outside, he looked around. They were high in the mountains, snow falling, about five inches of it on the ground.

The passengers, many of them upset, were gathering around the railroad crew, peppering them with questions. Micah wandered over, hand clutching the tender place where his head had struck the seat. He was slightly dizzy.

He stopped when he saw the ruptured and derailed freight car in which his horse had been carried.

"What happened?" he asked a man standing nearby.

"We almost all got killed," the man replied in an angry tone. "The train hit something on the track, that there fell-over tree, I think, and nigh got jarred clean off it. But that freight car there was the only one that actually derailed. We're danged lucky it didn't pull the rest of the train off with it."

"I had a horse being hauled in that car," Micah said.

"Uh-oh. You may have you a dead horse now."

Micah, ignoring his aching head, ran over to the shattered car and began peering around the wreckage, looking for his horse.

"Mister."

The speaker was a boy, blond-haired and shy-looking. Micah had noticed him earlier in the journey, seated with his mother.

"Yes, son?"

"You looking for your horse?"

"I am."

"It ain't in there. I saw it run loose, over that way." The boy pointed.

"Thank you, young man," Micah said. "I'll see if I can find him."

He headed off into the woods. Pausing, he looked back at the train. It would be a long time, he figured, before the train could be moved. He'd have plenty of time to find the horse, if it was to be found at all. The only question was whether there would be some other place on the train in which it could be carried.

Micah hesitated, though. What if he got lost? These mountains were a far cry from the familiar Kansas flatlands.

He shook off the worry. The horse couldn't

have roamed far. He'd find it quickly and get back to the train long before it moved off again.

Micah moved on into the rugged mountains.

In his California youth, Micah had become a fairly proficient tracker. Thus it did not take him long to detect sign of his horse, which he followed into the forested mountains. He felt certain he'd find his horse within a few minutes, check it over to make sure it had not been injured in the derailment, then take it back to the train, place it in one of the undamaged cars, and resume his journey.

After a while, however, he became less sure of the outcome. The sign seemed to vanish, and his horse was nowhere to be seen. He was surprised it had wandered this far in so short a time.

And how far, come to think of it, was this? He'd moved swiftly, concentrating on his tracking, and hadn't paid much attention to how far he'd come.

He paused, looking back toward the railroad. He could see nothing of it from here, nor hear any sounds of work going on to clear the ruined car from the tracks.

Micah felt a pang of worry. Maybe he should forget about the horse and just go back. What if they got the track cleared and the train went on without him? His baggage was on that train, all his clothing, goods, even his pistol and ammunition. He didn't want to be stranded out here with nothing in hand.

Yet he couldn't give up on the horse just yet. He wasn't a wealthy man. That horse had cost him a good deal. Besides, his wife and son were attached to it. He couldn't just sacrifice it. And what if it was injured? It would be cruel simply to abandon it out here in these mountains.

He pressed on, promising himself he would not go much farther.

Ahead . . . something had just moved on a hillside, going around an outcrop of rock just as Micah had glimpsed it. He wasn't sure, but it might have been the horse.

He advanced, picking his way along carefully, for the terrain was growing much rougher and steeper here. Gravel and other debris slid under his foot, and he fell with a grunt. He got to his feet again and proceeded even more carefully.

By the time he reached a position to allow him to see around the edge of the outcrop, whatever had created the movement he had seen had already vanished.

Micah felt a mounting irritation, not to mention a deepening worry. He'd come too far, and now wasn't sure he was quite the tracker he'd thought he was. The sign he'd been following might not have been left by his horse at all, and if it had been, it didn't matter now. He'd lost the trail long ago.

And he'd traveled much farther than he should have. Time to give up on the horse and head back to the train.

He turned, and his foot slipped on gravel again. This time he fell at a different angle, and rolled to a place where the hillside angled down at a very steep slope.

He tumbled down, rolling like a human boulder doing a one-man avalanche, pounding and slamming against stone in bruising fashion all the way to the bottom.

Chapter Twelve

Micah opened his eyes. He was lying on his left side, his body sprawled on stone, his cheek pressing against gravel. Blinking a few times, he tried to remember what had happened. Yes . . . he'd taken a tumble. Rolled down a slope . . .

Memory re-formed in his mind. The journey, the jolt on the tracks, the escape of his horse—he remembered it all now.

Cautiously he wiggled his toes, his fingers, then slowly sat up. His head hurt quite a lot. Turning slowly, he looked back up the slope down which he'd tumbled. Great day! Had he really fallen that far? He was lucky to be alive.

Micah said a brief prayer of thanks, then

looked around, beginning to notice that something had changed about the landscape.

The light. It fell at different angles now, and wasn't as bright as before. The sun was in the west, low on the horizon.

Could he really have lain there so long? He realized that he must have been unconscious. The day had passed and night was on its way.

The train . . .

Micah got up fast—and regretted it because of the way his head throbbed. He leaned against a sapling, letting a sudden burst of dizziness pass. Then he brushed off his clothing and made an assessment of his situation.

He was far away from the railroad tracks. Hours had passed. Either the train had moved on by now or his absence had been detected by the conductor and some sort of search launched.

He hoped the latter was the case. But by now, as late as it was, such a search might have been concluded. The conductor might be miles away by now, writing up a report at some distant railroad station about a passenger who vanished, with his horse, after the derailment.

"They probably figure I just rode off," Micah said aloud.

He began to panic, but got hold of himself. His situation was bad, no doubt about it, but not hopeless. He knew the direction in which the railroad lay. All he had to do was head south and eventually he'd run across it. He could find some shelter, pass the night. He could even hike up the tracks to the next stop if he felt up to it. He wasn't sure what the next stop was, or how far it was up the track, but eventually he'd reach it.

He wished he had his pistol with him, though. It was uncomfortable being out here without protection.

"Lord," he prayed aloud, "please watch over me. I've gotten myself into a real pickle."

No time to waste, he decided. The thing to do was reach the railroad. Who knows? Maybe he'd see a coming train and be able to flag it down, catch a ride. He'd probably find his baggage awaiting him at the next train station up the way.

Micah began hiking, but hiking soon turned to climbing. There was no way for him to advance far without getting back up the slope down which he'd fallen. He moved along the base of the slope until he reached a place where it wasn't as steep, and began clambering up.

Halfway to the top, he fell and rolled back down again. At the bottom he lay there, stunned and scared, and wondered if he'd broken any bones this time.

He had not, and said a prayer of thanks. But he felt greatly discouraged. It might take him until dark just to make it to the top of the slope again. He might have to spend a night out here in this wilderness alone and unarmed. And it was cold already, snow spitting down. He'd lost a lot of body heat lying on the ground as long as he had. At least he'd happened to fall into a place where the wind and terrain kept the ground mostly clear of snow accumulation. Had he lain directly in snow, he might have frozen to death.

He felt in his pockets . . . thank God! He had matches. At the very least he could build a fire.

He revised his plan. He'd reach the top of the slope, find a sheltered area, gather some wood, and build a fire. He'd feed it all night, keeping it hot and bright. If by chance there were searchers looking for him, they might see the blaze. If nothing else, it would keep him alive through the night and help avert predators.

Micah took a deep breath and made another go at the slope. He didn't allow himself to rush, and thought out every step before he took it. The sky was beginning to darken in the east, which worried him, but he didn't let it panic him. He'd be fine as long as he could get to the top in time to gather some firewood.

This time he made it, but the light was dimming fast. He walked swiftly southward until he found a natural recess among rocks. There the wind would be deflected and heat from a fire would reflect back off the surrounding rocks. Good.

Micah began gathering dead wood, as much as he could find, and carried it by armloads to his chosen camping place. He knew he'd have to have a lot of it to make it through the night, so he worked hard until it was too dark to see. Returning with the final armload to the rocky nook, he set fire to twigs and bark fragments, then began piling progressively larger sticks on the fire until at last he had a fine blaze going. The heat was marvelous. He settled back against a flat stone and enjoyed the fire, feeling quite comfortable.

When the fire died down somewhat, he picked up more sticks and replenished it. He began to feel sleepy, but decided to remain awake. It wouldn't be pleasant to let the fire go out and awaken to see himself facing off a bear or some other wild animal.

Hours passed. The fire burned and the supply of wood steadily diminished. Micah worried that he might run out, and lessened the size of the fire. At length he grew confident that indeed he'd have enough wood to see him through until morning.

Despite himself, he did sleep a little. He'd open his eyes at the sound of wood snapping in the blaze and realize he'd been dozing. He wished he had a big pot of coffee right now. And biscuits, dripping with butter. And a plateful of eggs, fried up just right like Alice always did them.

Whenever his next meal came, he'd enjoy it.

The fire was dimming again. Micah yawned

and reached over, grabbing another stick. He tossed it into the blaze . . . then came to his feet.

What he'd just put in the fire wasn't a stick. It was a bone. A human one, it appeared. Perhaps a thighbone.

Reflexively holding his breath, Micah began looking around. He pushed the remnants of his firewood supply to one side and examined the ground beneath it. The firelight wasn't bright enough to give him a good view, so he threw on some extra wood, then knelt to get a closer view of the ground.

He yelled and jumped back up again when he realized that staring back at him was a yellowed, crumbling human skull.

Micah scrambled completely out of the rocky enclave. Standing there in the snow, he wondered what a man is supposed to do when he discovers a corpse out in the wilderness. His first impulse was to hide it, but then he realized how irrational that was. He had nothing to do with this man's death and nothing to cover up.

When his burst of panic had subsided, he returned to where he had been and began to examine the bones as best he could in the dim and flickering light of the fire. How had this man died? How long had he been here? Micah's impression was that it must be quite a long time, but he knew nothing about rates of decay.

Gradually losing his squeamishness, he began

to pick about among the bones. There were quite a few of them, almost a full skeleton's worth, but badly scattered. Animals, he figured, had probably disturbed the corpse while there was still flesh on it upon which to feast. Thinking about that unsettled his stomach a little and caused him to make an inner vow never to die in the wilderness. Though he believed—and had declared in scores of sermons—that what happens to a body really doesn't matter because it is the soul that constitutes the true person, he had to admit that the thought of having his own bones scattered by beasts affected him more than he would have expected.

Micah put a little more wood on the fire and wished morning would come. He was eager to take a look at what he'd found with the full benefit of daylight.

Ten minutes later, he noticed a lightening of the eastern sky. The night had passed more quickly than he'd thought it would. He replenished the fire with the last of the wood and watched the sun rise, then set about to more closely examine the bones.

What drew his attention, however, was something that lay to the side of the bones, not visible until the daylight came. Micah knelt and picked up the holstered pistol he'd just spotted. It was a fine one, a Colt, with a bone handle gone slightly yellow. To his surprise, the holster had kept the pistol in good condition; there was hardly any rust at all. He checked and found it was loaded. The mechanism worked perfectly. Unloading the pistol, he snapped the trigger a few times.

He reloaded the pistol and noticed that almost all the cartridge loops on the gunbelt were full.

"I don't know who you were, my friend, but I'm grateful to have found your pistol," he said. "I feel much safer for having it."

Chapter Thirteen

Micah felt slightly qualmish about handling a gunbelt that had been around the waist of a corpse, but under the circumstances he was able to overcome it. The leather, having been exposed to the elements, was dark and stiff, but with some manipulation and rubbing he managed to make it somewhat supple again.

Micah had seldom worn a gun and usually didn't feel very comfortable with weapons. He had nothing against a man owning a gun, knew it to be a necessity in the West, but never had felt that preachers with guns were a natural fit. In these circumstances, though, being armed was a good thing.

Micah examined the bones, determining that indeed almost the full skeleton was present, though scattered about. He found a rusted knife, a few folded pieces of paper that bore smudged, unreadable markings, a couple of coins, an old matchcase, an ivory toothpick. Nothing more. Nothing to tell who this man had been.

Though in Micah's theology there was nothing to be gained by prayers for the dead, he felt the impulse to pray for this unknown person, this benefactor, in any case. He did so, interceding for the welfare of this man's soul, and the comfort of whatever loved ones he'd left behind. Micah realized that these people, whoever they were, could not know what had happened to this man. He wished he could identify him and find some way to deliver word of his death to those who needed to know it.

He considered burying the man, but decided not to. There might be legalities involved here he didn't know about. Someday someone knowledgeable of such matters might be able to examine this body and locale and learn who this man had been. It would probably never happen, though. These bones would probably never be seen again, only lie and molder away to nothing.

Micah was tired, hungry, a little scared, but glad to be armed and on the move. He began to walk southward toward the tracks.

When a sudden whiff of wood smoke reached

him, he stopped. His own fire was far behind him now, and out. Where could this smoke be coming from?

Curiosity led him to turn north. He'd not roam far, just far enough to find the origin of the smoke. The smell was stronger now. What if there was a forest fire? How fast would it spread?

He crossed a ridge. The smoky smell increased. But it wasn't so strong that Micah seriously suspected a forest fire. This was more like the smell of smoke near a campsite, or a town.

A town. Maybe there was a town back in these mountains, something off the rail line. He knew these mountains were home to many little mining communities, quick to rise and quick to vanish.

For the moment he forgot about the rail line. Sniffing the air, going in the direction from which the smoky smell came, he wandered well off his chosen course. His stomach rumbled as he thought he caught the scent of cooking meat mixed with the aroma of the smoke.

Abruptly, he came upon a road. It surprised him so that he stopped in his tracks and just stared at it. It was a narrow road, little more than a wagon trail. It wound around a hillside and out of sight. There were fresh wagon and horse tracks mixed with old ones.

Indeed that was meat he smelled. That could

only mean that the town, if town it was, was not far away.

Having his feet on a real road was pleasing. He lost the sense of being lost, and any immediate concern for returning to the railroad. He would visit this town, buy himself a good meal. Maybe he'd even find a room for the night and rest in a real bed. Sitting up in the snowy woods all night had worn him out.

He walked for less than a mile before seeing the first cabin. A man was chopping wood behind it, and paused to look Micah over as he strode up the road.

"Good day, friend," Micah called. "How are you?"

"Fine enough," the man replied. He seemed a little wary, but friendly as well. "And how are you?"

"Worn out, sir. I have some bad luck at the railroad." Briefly Micah related his adventure, omitting the part about the corpse and pistol. "So here I am with no horse, no baggage, and my nose guiding me to whatever lies ahead. Is there a town around the bend yonder?"

"There is. Not much of one."

"What's the name?"

"Levi Hill."

"Can't say I've heard of it."

"Just a little mining town. Nothing much."

"Is there a café?"

"A slop shop. That's what most of us call it. Stew and biscuits and the like."

"Sounds good enough for me."

Micah walked on, soon rounding the bend. There he stopped, and looked with some dismay on one of the most squalid towns he'd ever encountered.

There was no paint to be seen anywhere beyond that on a few crudely lettered commercial signs. Most of the bare wood buildings were splattered halfway up their fronts with mud from the rutted and pitted street. The street itself followed no clear line; it was more a muddy clearing between haphazardly located structures, all of which belched smoke from their stick-and-mud chimneys. The people were as dirty and colorless as the buildings. Even the horses tethered along the street seemed listless. The cleanest and most lively thing he saw, ironically, was a lone hog that wandered up the very center of the street.

Micah stepped aside to let the hog pass, then headed for the café. The smell of the meat was much stronger here, very heavy and greasy, nearly to the point of being unappealing.

At the edge of the café porch, Micah experienced a burst of momentary clarity. He realized how far from home he was, that in the course of this journey he had already lost his baggage, his horse and saddle, and his own pistol. Thank God he'd found a replacement for that, at least.

He also realized the absurdity of his mission. Merciful heaven, it wasn't only absurd, but undefined! He was searching for a murderer, a ghost from his own past, without any clear notion of how he would deal with him once he found him. This was no new realization, of course, but the light in which it struck him was. He saw clearly how nonsensical was his situation. He was the Reverend Micah Ward, for heaven's sake! A young and capable pastor who lived surrounded by his own small but productive lands and loving family, and by a congregation of devoted friends. What was he doing here?

He felt a sudden, overwhelming need to go home as quickly as possible. He would apologize to Alice and Flavius, then to his congregation. He would tell them he'd gone momentarily mad. He'd use his own foolishness as the source of a good dozen sermons.

But first, he'd eat. At least he could do that. He'd kept his money on his person, not in his baggage.

Chapter Fourteen

He ordered pork, eggs, and bread, and wolfed it all down in less than two minutes. Then he ordered a second round, and dined on it more slowly, taking time to examine his surroundings.

Amazing, how such things as cafés and shops and the like could spring up in the midst of nowhere. One day a wilderness, the next a town. This was the story of the American frontier, one that Micah had seldom taken time to ponder. Now that he did, he was quite struck by its significance. This transformation from wildness to civilization—of a sort—seemed to Micah quite a good metaphor for the salvation of a soul. Yes, he could use that, as soon as he got back to his home and his pulpit.

Someone slid into the chair across from him. A smiling face, feminine and beautiful, framed by curled, auburn hair. This stranger gave him an instant impression of childishness, until he looked into her eyes. Despite her smile, her eyes were cold, hardened.

She laid a pistol on the table before him.

"You dropped this."

He looked at it. Indeed it was the pistol he'd found with the dead man.

"I'll be . . . I didn't know."

"It fell out of your holster while you were eating, and you didn't even notice. I never saw a man so wrapped up in his food. It made quite a clunking noise. Didn't you hear it?"

"I didn't," he admitted.

"A man who eats like that, I figure, must not have eaten for a long time."

"It had been a few hours."

She leaned a little closer and let her finger trail along the pistol. "Maybe a man who hasn't eaten in a long time hasn't done some other things in a long time, either."

The religiously centered life that Micah had lived had protected him from the side of life that was now facing him, and for several moments he honestly failed to recognize what was happening. When the realization struck, his eyes widened and he sat back. "Miss . . . I don't think it's at all appropriate, what you seem to be implying."

Now she was the surprised one. "What?" She laughed. "What are you? Some kind of preacher?"

"As a matter of fact, I am."

She stared at him as if he'd just grown a second pair of eyes. "You lying to me?"

"No."

She laughed again, scooted her chair back, and waved toward Micah. "Did you hear that?" she said to the general population of the room. "He says he's a preacher!"

They all laughed. Micah was puzzled. It was funny, being a preacher? Had these people never encountered a preacher before?

Maybe they hadn't.

Lord, he thought, how sheltered have I been?

The young woman said, "Charlie, come over here and meet the preacher!"

A grinning, egg-bald man of indeterminate age came over, limping on a left leg that was a good eight inches shorter than the right one. He stuck out his hand at Micah. "Howdy, Preacher! Charlie Johnson."

Micah shook the hand. "Charlie."

"You really a preacher?"

"Yes."

"Well! Save my soul for me, Preacher!"

"I can't save anybody's soul."

"I thought that's what you preachers did. I thought you went around looking for sinners and saving their souls. Speaking of sinners, what do you think of Missy here?" He touched the girl on her shoulder. "Missy here knows sinning up and down. She can sin with the best of them, let me tell you! All for no more than a coin or two. She's the best sinner I ever—"

He cut off. His eyes had just fallen on the pistol lying on the table. The smile vanished, and he looked from the pistol to Micah and back to the pistol again, several times over. "I'll be damned," he whispered.

Micah was utterly confused now, and also repelled. He wasn't accustomed to people or conversations of this sort. He reached over, took the pistol, and holstered it.

"That's your pistol," Charlie said, very serious all at once.

"Yes . . ."

"Has it always been your pistol?"

"No."

"The man you got it from . . . was he alive or dead?"

"Dead. Why do you ask?"

Charlie laughed again, but it was a very false laugh. Nervous, respectful, maybe fearful. Micah realized that Charlie was suddenly very mindful of not offending him. Charlie backed away, hands up with palms facing Micah, waving side to side. "Sorry I bothered you, Preacher. I didn't know . . . I thought you were, you know, a real preacher."

"What are you acting that way for, Charlie?" Missy asked.

"Come on, Missy. Come on. Let's leave this man alone. We don't want to be bothering him, no, no."

The girl looked confused as Charlie pulled her away. Micah watched as Charlie talked to her in a whisper in the far corner of the room. She kept glancing his way, and suddenly her expression changed. Her last glance his way was one of astonishment, as if he were the president and she'd just recognized him.

Micah had had enough of this. He stood and left money on the table, then walked over to the proprietor. "Where might a man rent a room for the night in this town?"

"Well, there's a room with a bed upstairs. The lady who used to be in there run off a month ago."

"I'll take it, if you'll give me a reasonable cost."

"Jimbo . . ." The speaker was Charlie, who came to the proprietor and briefly pulled him aside and whispered in his ear. The proprietor cocked up a brow and studied Micah with a look of surprise.

"I can give you the best kind of rate—no charge," he said.

Micah was befuddled. "Free?"

"That's right."

"Because I'm a preacher? Is that it?"

Charlie and Jimbo thought that one was funny. "That's it, sure enough. Because you're a preacher."

Micah smiled and nodded, said thank you, and headed up the stairs. It was morning, but he'd hardly rested the night before and was eager for sleep. And to get out of this rather odd and unexpectedly uncomfortable setting.

He'd stay in Levi Hill long enough to get a little rest, but after that he'd move on as fast as possible.

Chapter Fifteen

After Micah had gone up the stairs, a man who had been inconspicuously seated at a table in the rear corner stood and approached Charlie and Jimbo.

"Begging your pardon, gentlemen, but I'd like to talk to you," he said. He reached into his pocket and produced two business cards. "My name's Brandon Rhoton. I'm a writer for the *American Crime Chronicle*. I'd like to know a little more about what I just saw happening here."

"You write for the *American Crime Chronicle*?" Charlie said.

"That's right. And I'm in a bit of a bind. I'm overdue in providing a story for the next edition, and I missed providing one at all for the past two months. So you can be sure, gentlemen, that I'm very interested in what I just witnessed." He paused and smiled. "Do I smell a possible story here?"

"You do . . . if you want to know about the man who killed Diamond Willie."

"Diamond Willie the gunfighter?"

"Yep. You really do write for the *American Crime Chronicle*? No lying?"

"No lying." Rhoton produced a notepad from under his coat, and a stubby pencil. "I'd like to take a few notes, for my memory. You're telling me that the man who just went up those stairs is the killer of Diamond Willie?"

Having someone taking notes of his words made Charlie feel important, and he took on an instant tone of authority. "Diamond Willie vanished a year ago. Nobody knew what happened to him, but Diamond Willie being Diamond Willie, everybody figured he'd been killed by some other gunfighter. He had enemies all over, and a reputation that a lot of gunmen would like to take over for themselves."

"So what makes you say that man killed Diamond Willie?"

"Because I know Diamond Willie's pistol. I seen him showing it off a couple of times when he and me were in Denver at the same time. I played cards with Diamond Willie once . . . almost was a friend of his. I know the pistol he carried. There was a mark he'd made on the bone handle."

"And that pistol . . ."

"Was the one that the preacher had today," Charlie said firmly.

"No question about it?"

"Nope. That preacher up there killed Diamond Willie."

"Which I'd say means he's no authentic preacher, surely."

"Most likely 'Preacher' is his gunfighting name. Like Diamond Willie going by Diamond Willie instead of whatever his real name was."

Rhoton chewed the end of the pencil, thinking. "So we've got a new gunfighter roaming around. Calls himself a preacher, and uses the gun of Diamond Willie."

"Surely seems that way to me."

"Me too," Jimbo the proprietor threw in, not wanting to be left out of this story.

"And so we've got a mystery . . . just who is Preacher the gunfighter? How and when did he kill Diamond Willie? And why has he waited this long to show himself?"

"Good questions," Charlie said.

"Yes," Jimbo agreed. "Good questions."

"And most of all, a good story," Rhoton said. "The best story I've run across in God knows how long."

"You're going to put this in the newspaper?"

"Oh, yes. Yes indeed."

"You going to talk to the preacher?"

"I just might." He laughed and slapped the notepad against the heel of his hand. "You know, I had a feeling I was right to come here! Something told me to search out this godforsaken little mining town! It didn't make sense, but I knew that I'd find the story I needed here. Just knew it. What's the day? What's the day?"

"Tuesday."

"No, the date!"

"The third."

"Good. Good. That gives me the time I need. I can talk to this preacher, get my story written, get to a telegraph station."

"You going to put my name in there?" Charlie asked.

"Of course." In fact, the weaselly Rhoton didn't care who Charlie was or plan to give credit to him in any way.

"Me too?" Jimbo added.

"Certainly."

"I'll go up and see him," Missy said. She'd been listening to the conversation. "I can make him tell whatever you want him to tell."

"I don't think you're his type, honey," Rhoton said. "If you were, he'd have you with him already. Coffee. I want some coffee. I'm ready to start a little writing."

* * *

Micah rolled over in his bed and opened his eyes. He stared at an unfamiliar wall and window, through which a diminished light, like that of twilight, pierced dirty glass and even dirtier curtains.

Odd sounds and music came from below, muffled; he realized that it was this that had woken him. He felt quite confused for half a minute, then remembered that he was upstairs above a café in a remote Colorado mining town.

He sat up, grinning and shaking his head. What an odd place for him to be! Once again the whole unlikely nature of his mission struck him. He felt far away from home, and lonely, but not particularly unhappy at the moment. The rest had done him good.

A glance out the window, however, revealed that he had slept the day away. The sun was westering. It would be pointless to attempt to walk to the railroad tonight.

He'd have to speak to the proprietor about spending the night in this room. Not that sleep would be likely. He'd gotten hours of sleep already, and the café downstairs would probably be noisy long into the night. He'd noticed the bar there earlier, and surmised that what was a café by day was probably more a saloon by night.

He went to the mirror and combed his hair. He ran his hand across his whiskers and pondered his changing appearance. A few more days without shaving, a little more time on the road, and he'd hardly be recognizable as the Reverend Micah Ward.

Unexpectedly, that thought brought a twinge of excitement. He thought of the girl downstairs who had offered herself to him. In all his life, at least since his youth in the wild California mining camps, he'd never encountered a prostitute. Had never been around the sort of folks who drink and fight and talk crudely. He'd been in the protective circle of the church almost perpetually.

He stared in the mirror, thinking things he shouldn't as he gazed into the reflection of his eyes. . . .

With an effort of will he shrugged it off. No! No. He'd not let the occasion of isolation and separation from his family cause him to fall away. He'd resist temptation.

Still staring at himself in the mirror, he quoted scripture: " 'There has no temptation taken you but such as is common to man. But God is faithful, and will not suffer you to be tempted above that which ye are able, but will with the temptation provide a way of escape, so that ye may be able to bear it.' " He leaned closer to his own reflection. "In other words, Micah Ward, you've got no excuse to not behave yourself."

The noise below was growing louder. Sounds

of revelry. The piano in the corner hammering loudly, mostly out of tune. Unfamiliar sounds to a man who heard mostly hymns as piano music.

Micah was hungry. Maybe the café continued to function even after the saloon opened.

Straightening his clothing, Micah went to the door. . . .

He thought of something and hesitated. "No," he said to himself. "I don't need it." He started to open the door again, hesitated another time, then gave in.

Need it or not, he'd feel better with the gunbelt strapped around his waist. He worried about that. Was he losing his faith in God to protect him? Or was wearing a gun and dining in a saloon part of some game of pretend he was playing with himself? Was he enjoying toying around on the edges of a lifestyle he'd never known personally but preached against a hundred times?

"You think a little too much for your own good, Micah," he counseled himself. "You want to wear the pistol, wear the pistol. There's apparently no law against it in this town."

He walked down the stairs into the room below.

Chapter Sixteen

He noticed three things, one right after another.

The first was that the room was surprisingly crowded. A good dozen or more people, quite a group for such a small town, and three more entered even as he descended.

The second was that he seemed to attract much attention as he made his own entrance. He knew right away that he'd been discussed during his absence. Maybe it was a true novelty to have a preacher in this place.

The third thing was that he recognized two faces among the people. Two of the men who had been ready to burn that dog at the train station were here. The one whose nose he'd broken was not one of them; these were simply two of the ones who'd been with him. He saw that they recognized him even as he recognized them.

Micah descended the stairs and headed for the bar. He noticed that his pistol seemed to attract many glances. He couldn't figure out why; several of the men here bore side arms.

Micah went to the bar. "I'm looking for some supper."

"Café's closed. Sorry. We only run that during the daytime. If you want a drink, though . . ."

A man slid up to the bar beside Micah and said to the barkeep, "If this man wants supper, I'd suggest you change your policy and give it to him. I don't think Preacher here is a man to be trifled with."

Micah looked curiously at the stranger. "You know I'm a preacher?"

"I do, sir."

"And what are you?"

"I'm a writer, sir. For the *American Crime Chronicle*. Have you heard of us?"

"Oh, yes."

"Good. Good."

"How do you know about me?" Micah asked.

"I'm a journalist, sir. I listen to things. Ask questions. Put together surmises."

"And what have you surmised about me?"

"That a man in your profession wouldn't come to a place like this without a reason."

"Well, in a manner of speaking, I suppose you're right. I don't believe that anything happens without a reason."

"That may be true, sir."

"What's your name?" Micah asked.

"Rhoton."

"And mine is—"

"No! No. Don't tell me. A mystery is better. Always. The readers go for that, you see. Preacher. That's all the name needs. Just Preacher. Traveling the West, bearing that very special and significant pistol . . . and doing what? Looking for someone, I'd wager."

"As a matter of fact, I am. But about my pistol . . . what makes it 'special and significant'?"

Rhoton threw back his head and laughed. "Don't we all know."

"I'm not sure what you mean."

"When you took that from its former owner, he was dead, correct?"

"That's right."

"Quite a trophy."

"It wasn't a trophy. Just a useful and needed tool."

"Tell me, Preacher: How did you get that cross-shaped scar on your face? And who are you looking for?"

Micah wondered why this man was so curious about him. But experience had made him prone to be open about himself to encourage others to be open with him. "How I got the scar is something I'm not all that eager to talk about. And who I'm looking for, though it's no one else's business, is a man named Tipton Barth."

Rhoton's face changed. "Tipton Barth!" he said. "I'll be damned!"

"Not unless you choose to be," Micah answered, always ready to spread the message to which he'd devoted his life. "There's a way to escape that for all of us."

Two others stepped up, the pair from the train station. To Rhoton they said, "This is quite a man you're talking to here. We both saw him down a man right on a train station platform."

"Do tell!" Rhoton pulled out his notepad and scribbled on it.

"Hello, Preacher," the man said to Micah.

"Hello," Micah replied, wary. Who would have imagined he'd run into any of the train station gang again?

Micah didn't quite understand all of this attention, particularly that of the journalist, and was ready to find some food.

"Is there a place around here that sells food?" he asked.

"Gerty James serves up supper on her back porch across town," the bartender said.

"I'll be going there, then," Micah said.

"He told us he was a preacher," the man from the train station said.

Rhoton laughed. "Oh, yes. Some kind of preacher a gunfighter is!"

Micah frowned at him. "A gunfighter? What gives you that notion? I am a preacher."

They laughed. Micah, puzzled, decided explanation wasn't worth the effort.

He obtained directions to Gerty James's place from the bartender and left, feeling almost every eye upon him.

"I don't care what he says—he's a gunfighter, all right," Rhoton said after Micah was gone. "A man doesn't have the gun of Diamond Willie on him and not be a gunfighter. Mark my words: That man there gunned down Diamond Willie. And now he's looking for Tipton Barth, a man any sane man would do anything to avoid. He's a gunfighter, no question of it."

"He's good with his fists, too," one of the train station men said. "You should have seen how he busted Horace's nose."

"Busted his nose?" Rhoton said. "I thought you said he gunned him down."

"No, no. Just fists."

Rhoton swore. "Gunning down would be better for my purposes. What the hell . . . I'll write it that it was a gunfight."

"Write it? What do you mean?"

"I'm a journalist. A writer. I'm getting ready to reveal the story of Preacher, the killer of the infamous Diamond Willie, to the reading world."

"No lie!"

"I'll lie as need be. My kind of journalism doesn't exactly require devotion to the truth. Not completely, anyway."

"You say he killed Diamond Willie?"

"That's Willie's pistol he carries. How else would he have got it? Diamond Willie killed seven men in fair fights, and that many more again in fights that maybe weren't so fair. Nobody would have been able to get Diamond Willie's pistol from him short of killing him for it."

"You reckon he aims to kill Tipton Barth, too?"

"That would be my guess. That's what I intend to write. Why else would he be looking for such a one as Barth if not to kill him? I hope he succeeds. Barth is the worse scum you'll ever find. And besides, it would make a devil of a story."

"What if he really is just a preacher?"

"Hah! That's no preacher. I'll guarantee you that. That's a gunfighter, and I'm just about to make him famous," Rhoton said. "Half my story's already written. I'll wire it in tomorrow, and within a week, everybody who reads the *American Crime Chronicle* will be talking about Preacher, the mysterious new gunfighter with the T-shaped scar on his face who's roaming the mountains of Colorado and gunning for Tipton Barth."

Chapter Seventeen

The food at Gerty's was delicious, though the filthiness of the woman as well as that of her place was enough to make Micah glad he hadn't watched the meal being prepared. Sometimes it was just best not to know.

The only other diners were two enormously fat men who, Micah gathered, were nightly customers of Gerty's informal restaurant, plus a couple of somber miners and an elderly woman Gerty called Aunt Hannah. Nobody except Gerty had much to say, and she had plenty. She jabbered throughout the meal, talking over a wide variety of news and opinions and rumors. Micah grew weary listening to her, then realized she might possess some knowledge that could help him.

"Beg your pardon, ma'am, but could I ask you something?" Micah asked during one of Gerty's rare pauses for breath.

"Why, speak on up!"

"Have you ever heard of a man named Tipton Barth?"

Gerty dropped into silence, and the others at the table all looked up at Micah.

"Oh, I've heard of that devil, yes sir," she said, solemn.

"Well, do you know where he might be found?"

One of the fat men said, "Beg pardon, friend, but why would anyone want to find Tipton Barth?"

"I . . . I didn't say I wanted to find him. I was just wondering if he really was in these parts."

"Are you a law officer?" the fat man asked.

"Not exactly. It's just a matter of interest to me. Curiosity."

"Are you a friend of his?"

"No. Anything but a friend."

"Thank the Lord for that. If you were friendly with that son of Satan, you'd not be a man I want to share a table with."

Gerty seized control of the conversation again. "That's right, sir. You're best not even to think of Tipton Barth. God only knows what kind of divine judgment was being done on this world when those two were created. One of them, Leroy, has gone onto his eternal punishment, thank God. But Tipton remains. Still as foul and wicked as ever, they say, and a danger to every citizen. May God take him to join his brother soon."

Micah, who had nearly lost his resolve to go after Barth already, felt his resolve decline even more. "They tell me he is seen sometimes around Greentree."

"I've heard the same," one of the miners said. "They say he killed a woman and child there once. They say he and some of his ilk still linger in the area quite a lot. Like ghosts in the hills. Some folks are afraid to prospect around Greentree for fear of Barth and his gang."

"I can't say I blame them." Micah ventured a little bit of self-revelation. "I had an encounter with Tipton Barth many years ago, myself. In mining country, but not here. It was California, during the rush."

"That's a long time back."

"Yes. But Barth was then the same thing he is now. A murderer. He killed a man named Jim Sneed and was put on trial for it. If he'd been convicted, he'd have been hanged."

"And why wasn't he convicted?"

Micah paused. "The story is that a witness who could have identified him as the killer was threatened by Tipton's brother. So he didn't tell the truth, and Tipton Barth went free."

They all thought about that. "Think of the lives that would have been saved if he'd been hanged."

"Yes," Micah said. "I have thought about that. Many times."

Aunt Hannah looked at him in a way that made Micah think she had read more between his words than had the others. "You ain't thinking of looking for him after all these years, are you?"

Micah's conscience wouldn't let him lie, but he didn't want to give a strictly straight answer, either. "It would take quite a strong motivation to want to find a man like that!" he said.

"Amen," said one of the miners. "I say let him stay far away from me. It's why I don't venture up toward Greentree. Them's dangerous climes. A lot worse than here."

"Well, I'll stay away. But . . . if somebody did want to find Tipton Barth, how would be the best way to go about it?"

"The best way . . . well, I reckon just get out the word that you're after him. Wanting to do him in, you know. He'd come looking for you then. The man's got a lot of pride in his reputation."

Micah finished his meal, telling himself he'd indeed best give up this notion of searching for Barth. He'd go back to his home and family and church and let things be like they used to be.

And when Jack Tower came around . . . well, he'd just not look him in the eye.

Micah rose to leave. Aunt Hannah lifted her withered face toward him and said, "Young man

. . . God go with you. You are the sword of the Lord. The sword of the Lord."

Micah mumbled an uncertain reply, paid for his food, and returned to the saloon. Passing through the barroom, he once again received many stares and evoked many whispers. He climbed the stairs to his room and took a glance back into the main room.

Rhoton was at a rear table, writing furiously on his pad, so lost in his creativity that he hadn't even noticed Micah's return.

It took a very long time for the noise in the saloon to subside, and an even longer time yet for Micah to go to sleep.

Micah tried to pay the proprietor for his room the next morning, but the man continued to refuse it. Micah argued only briefly, then simply thanked the man and prepared to leave. He was ready to get out of this town.

"By the way, that story's been wrote, and Mr. Rhoton's gone on to wire it in as quick as he can get to a telegraph," the proprietor said as Micah was leaving. "You might run across him out on the road."

"That's interesting," Micah said, though really he wasn't much interested and hoped he didn't run across Rhoton on the road. He'd paid little attention to the scribbler, who seemed a pretentious and unimportant fellow. If Rhoton was a real journalist at all, he couldn't be much of one if he was hanging around backwater mining towns like this one.

Micah thought about the fact that he'd been mistaken for a gunfighter and smiled. Alice would think that was funny. But Alice was a long way off. His life back in Kansas was a long way off, too.

Here, where no one knew him, he could well be a gunfighter, or a miner, or a lawman. He was just one more lone drifter, unknown to anyone.

But God knew him, he reminded himself. It was still his duty to behave as he should.

He left Levi Hill and walked back into the mountains. As he passed near the area where he'd found the skeleton, he realized he'd done nothing about officially reporting the find. There had been no law in Levi Hill that he'd seen, no official town structure of authority. Nothing he could do.

He trudged on, wondering how long it would take to reach the railroad.

A mile or so out, Micah stopped and turned. He thought he'd heard someone behind him. He waited to see if anyone would round the bend, but no one did, and now that he listened more closely, he could hear nothing.

Even so, he was sure he'd heard something. Maybe that journalist hadn't gone ahead after all, but was behind him. That made Micah want to hurry on. He didn't want to become a fellow traveler of Rhoton's.

Chapter Eighteen

The wrecked railroad car was still there, lying beside the track. Micah looked around for his horse again, just in case it had wandered back this way. But it hadn't. Even if he did find it, his saddle was gone, along with his baggage.

Part of Micah was ready to head back to Kansas right now, but he hadn't made up his mind about what to do. For the sake of the baggage and the saddle alone, he felt compelled to go on toward Greentree. If his possessions were being held for him by the railroad, as he hoped, they probably were stashed up at the next railroad stop.

Micah walked up the track, which climbed up

a steady grade and also curved around the side of a hill. The view was frequently spectacular, inspiring him to softly sing hymns as he trudged along. Eventually he grew so out of breath that the hymn singing stopped and he put his full concentration into his exertions.

Sometimes he would stop to rest, other times because he couldn't get over the notion that someone was traveling behind him. Yet he never spotted anyone. If he was being followed, his tracker was being careful not to get very close.

It was unnerving, and Micah hoped he was merely the victim of an overactive imagination.

The railroad tracks led him to a little whistle-stop named Borden. There was no town here, just a tiny train station with a water tank, a house or two nearby, and a small trading post that also sold sandwiches.

Micah went straight for the trading post and ordered food. He ate ravenously and drank several cups of coffee. All this walking made a man need plenty of fuel to keep going.

As he downed his last bite, he looked out of the trading post window and saw a man, bearing a rifle, come walking up the tracks the same way he had. Micah froze in midchew. So someone had been following him!

He looked closely at the man. He was some distance away and hard to see, but Micah was sure he'd seen that face in the saloon back at Levi Hill.

Micah wondered if he'd been truly followed, or if he and this man simply shared the same route by coincidence. He hoped it was the latter.

After paying for his food, Micah left, took advantage of a nearby privy, then headed to the train station. The man from the Levi Hill saloon was on the porch, rolling a cigarette. He didn't glance up as Micah walked past him and through the door.

The station master was freeing a dead rat from a trap and cussing the fact that cold weather drove the rodents indoors. His listener was a man seated on a stool in the corner, reading a newspaper. Micah paid the fellow no heed.

"I'm looking for some baggage that might have been left off by the last Greentree-bound train," Micah said. "A carpetbag and maybe a saddle." He briefly explained the derailment and how he'd managed to become separated from the train.

"Matter of fact, there is a carpetbag," the station master said, wiping his hands on his pants to get off the essence of deceased rat. "No saddle, though."

"I feared that," Micah said. It gave him a rather sickly feeling in the pit of his stomach. That saddle was one of his best possessions. Or had been.

"What color's the carpetbag?" the station master asked.

"Red. Solid."

"What color handle?"

"Black."

"All righty. Just had to check to be sure you and the bag really do go together. I've got it stowed in the back. Hang on."

The station master entered a large rear closet and began banging around in there, unseen but noisy.

A hand touched Micah's shoulder, startling him. He pivoted.

"Whoa, sir, sorry to startle you!" It was Rhoton, the journalist. "Just wanted to say hello."

"Right. Well . . . hello. What brings you here?"

"The telegraph line. It's my avenue of communication with my publication, you see. I wire in my stories."

"I see."

"You've lost baggage, I gather?"

"That's right. But I think I've found it again."

The station master emerged with a red carpetbag in hand. "This look to be the one?"

"I think so."

Micah opened the bag and glanced inside. There at the top of the contents was his gray shirt, just where he'd left it. It appeared the bag's contents had not been bothered.

"This is it," Micah said. "Thank you, sir."

"No problem. Sorry about the saddle. I can assure you, if it was took, it wasn't took by nobody associated with the railroad. It may be you'll find it awaiting you at Greentree. There's a warehouse there where they store bigger items that get separated from their owners on trains."

"I see." Micah sighed. He'd been indecisive about continuing to Greentree or just turning back home and dropping his quest for Tipton Barth. Now it seemed he'd have to go onto Greentree simply to find his saddle.

"When's the next train to Greentree?" he asked.

"Not until tomorrow afternoon."

"Tomorrow—"

"Well!" Rhoton said. "That gives us plenty of time to talk!"

Micah glanced at him. Something about Rhoton, who wore a seedy suit and an even more seedy smile, annoyed him greatly. The idea of spending a day in conversation with him was not at all inspirational.

"Is Greentree the next stop up the track?"

"That's right. Ten miles."

"Micah pondered. He'd walked greater distances many a time, though admittedly not in the thin air of mountain country. "A steep climb?"

"Oh, no. We're on nearly the same level as Greentree right here. Just a shallow climb."

"Thank you." He'd made his decision. He'd walk the rest of the way and thus avoid an afternoon with Rhoton and the necessity of an overnight wait.

"Do you have some time to talk?" Rhoton said. He had his notepad out, and Micah recalled the fellow's illusion that Micah was some sort of mysterious gunfighter.

"I'm afraid not, sir," Micah repied. "I'm moving on."

Rhoton looked disappointed. "Well. In that case, I suppose I'll have to say farewell, then."

He glanced down at the pistol holstered on Micah's hip. "The pistol of Diamond Willie! My, my. Can you at least tell me where Diamond Willie is now?"

"The man who last owned this pistol is in the hands of the Lord," Micah said. "Now, good day, and all the best to you." Micah turned and carried his carpetbag out the door, gladly leaving Rhoton behind.

The Levi Hill stranger was still on the porch, staring off at the mountains. Again he ignored Micah.

Micah strode out across the station yard to the tracks and began walking up them toward Greentree. He glanced back as he was about to go out of sight of the station.

The man on the porch was still sitting there, rolling another cigarette.

Micah was relieved. Apparently he wasn't being followed after all.

Chapter Nineteen

Refreshed by food and glad to have his bag again, Micah walked energetically for nearly two miles before he was at last forced to slow down. The mountain atmosphere certainly wasn't as rich as what he was accustomed to, and the blasted bag was growing heavier in his hand with every step. It felt as if it was loaded with bricks. Just what had he packed that was so heavy?

Ready for a rest, he veered off the tracks and sat down on a log, letting his breathing slow and his heart quit hammering so hard. He sat the carpetbag at his feet, glad to be momentarily free of the burden.

A noise . . .

He turned, looking back down the track. He couldn't see far, because the tracks made a curve, but it sounded as if . . .

No. Why would anyone follow him? Probably just some animal crossing the tracks. He'd left that stranger still sitting on the porch at the train station.

Of course, he might have gotten up and followed as quickly as Micah was out of sight. . . .

Micah listened again but heard nothing. No reason to worry, he decided. He was just letting this Tipton Barth business get him edgy.

Micah picked up the carpetbag. It did seem overly heavy. Putting it onto his lap, he opened it and pulled out the shirt.

He looked inside. "I'll be!" he said aloud.

This wasn't his bag at all! It was of the same color and nearly identical design, and happened to have been packed with a gray shirt on the top of the stack, but beneath that, everything was different.

And no wonder the bag was heavy. The most noticeable part of its contents was a revolver and a big box of ammunition. The revolver was small, the kind a man might carry in a shoulder-rig holster, but it was heavy. Micah pulled it out and studied it. It was loaded. He laid it down on the log beside him and continued to dig through the bag.

He found numerous personal items, such as a

matchcase, a shaving kit, and a tobacco box. There was also a snap-latch money pouch, marked with the name "Johnny Cole" and seemingly quite stuffed.

Micah looked inside. The money pouch contained a thick roll of bills, tied up with a piece of twine. Micah slipped the twine loose and let the bills unroll themselves in his hand. Most of them were fifty-dollar bills, plus several hundred-dollar bills. There was at least a thousand dollars here.

Poor Johnny Cole, whoever he was. Micah had thought his own loss was significant, but Cole had lost a lot more than Micah had when this carpetbag went out of hand.

"Well! Looks like I'll be gaining more than just a famous pistol here today!"

Micah came to his feet, dumping the carpetbag on the ground in the process. The bills he clutched in his fist by reflex.

"That's a lot of money, Preacher," said the man Micah had last seen on the station house porch. "You steal that from somebody you gunned down? Diamond Willie, maybe?"

The stranger had a pistol leveled on Micah and a wicked grin on his face.

"What do you want from me?"

"Very simple. I want that pistol you carry. I want the pistol of Diamond Willie. So why don't you loose that gunbelt, real slow."

Micah stooped slowly and laid the money on the ground by his feet. He then stood and unbuckled the gunbelt.

"Toss it over here."

Micah complied, the gunbelt plopping on the ground at the pistoleer's feet.

The man laughed. "Diamond Willie's own pistol! Imagine that! Diamond Willie killed a lot of men with that there pistol. It's a famous weapon. The man who carries it gains a reputation with it. Tell me this: Where did Diamond Willie die?"

"The man who owned that pistol lies dead in the wilderness not far from Levi Hill. Whether his name is Willie I couldn't tell you."

"You must be some kind of gunfighter to have downed Diamond Willie. They say you couldn't see the man's hand move when he'd draw, so fast he was."

"I'm no gunfighter. And you don't understand. Diamond Willie, if that's who he was, was already—"

"Shut up. It don't matter now. It'll be me who gets the credit for killing Willie, and I'll make up my own story about how it happened. Diamond Willie ain't been seen in over a year that I know of, and I can tell any tale I want. Tell me this, though: Do you really call yourself Preacher?"

"I am a preacher."

"I'll bet you are. Did you say any Bible verses to Willie when you blasted him into hell?"

"My friend, you have a very wrong understanding of this whole situation."

"Do I, now? Well, like I said, it don't matter. I can make up my own story . . . once you're out of the way."

"What do you mean?"

"I intend to claim credit for killing Diamond Willie. There was a bounty on his head, you know. A big one. I produce that pistol, and I may stand a chance of gaining it. If nothing else, I'll gain the reputation that goes with killing so famous a gunfighter. But I can't very well leave you to go around telling your own version of the tale, can I?"

"Mister, I have a wife, a son. If you intend to harm me . . ."

"Harm? Not harm. I intend to kill you. We're all alone out here, Preacher. Nobody will know how it happened. Who knows? Maybe there's a bounty on your head, too!"

Instinct made Micah move. Somehow, a moment before it happened, he sensed that the man was going to pull the trigger. He threw himself to the left as the shot blasted, so close that he felt the hot sting of the expelled gunpowder. The bullet narrowly missed him.

The man swore and cocked the pistol again. Micah's hand swept down and scooped up the pistol he'd removed from the carpetbag and laid on the log. Still acting by instinct, he lifted it and fired, simultaneous with his attacker's second shot.

That second bullet also missed Micah, though it cut a little crease in the sleeve of his coat.

Micah's randomly fired shot, however, was more effective. It caught the gunman in the right hand, taking off two fingers at the top knuckles and making him fling his own pistol aside. It lay smoking on the ground while the man, howling in pain, gripped his bleeding right hand with his left one and staggered backward.

Micah, holding the pistol he'd just fired for the first time in his life, gaped, amazed at the shot he'd just pulled off. The Lord surely must have guided that bullet, for Micah hadn't even had time to aim.

The man lifted a pallid face and looked at Micah with the expression of a man expecting to die at any moment.

"Just make it fast . . . that's all I ask. Don't gut-shoot me, please!"

Micah lowered the pistol. "I don't intend to shoot you at all. I wouldn't have shot you then if I hadn't been forced to."

"You ain't going to kill me?"

"No. I just want you to go away."

The man, despite his pain, laughed in relief. "Bless you, mister. Bless you! You ain't going to kill me, really?"

"Really. Just . . . just go away. Don't ever let me

see you again." The preacher in Micah emerged for a moment. "And put this kind of thing behind you. You don't want to be a murderer. You don't want to kill a man for something so foolish as to possess some other murderer's pistol. Go on. Put sin behind you and turn to the Lord."

"You really do sound like a preacher!"

"I told you, I am one. How's your hand? You won't bleed to death, will you?"

"No. I got two fingers gone, though. God, it hurts!"

"Go back to the train station. They can patch you up."

"Bless you, Preacher. Thank you for not killing me. You shot off my fingers, but you could have just as easy put that bullet through my head."

It disgusted Micah to see a man who moments before had been ready to kill him and gloat about it now fawning and gushing before him.

"Get away from here. I forgive you for what you tried to do, but I have no desire to lay eyes on you anymore."

"Can I get my pistol that I flung over yonder?"

"I'm not that kind of fool, my friend. Just go on and be grateful you're still alive and not beyond hope."

"Can I look for my fingers?"

"They won't be useful to you now. Just go on."

The man, bleeding and holding his hand, turned and ran down the tracks and nearly out of sight. He turned, though, and called back: "What's your name, Preacher?"

Micah had no interest in this man knowing who he was. He might have just told the fellow to shut up and keep running, but he was shaken by the realization he'd just shot a man. So he impulsively did something uncharacteristic: He lied. The name he'd found in the carpetbag flashed back to mind, and he called back, "Johnny Cole."

The man turned and ran out of sight.

Micah sat down on the log again, letting out a long, slow breath. He was shaking now, feeling faint. He thanked God he was still alive, and wished he'd never left Kansas.

Chapter Twenty

The station master pulled his watch from his vest pocket and looked at it with a frown.

"Mr. Rhoton, sir, I think you've tied up my telegraph line long enough," he said, snapping the cover down again. "When will you be finished?"

Rhoton clicked the keys a few more times, stood, and tipped his hat. "All finished, sir. And I thank you."

"I'm not really supposed to do that, you know. Letting somebody unofficial use my telegraph, I mean."

"Would you have wanted to transmit so lengthy a story yourself?" Rhoton asked. He was feeling smug and satisfied just now. He'd just wired in a story—like most he wrote, one-third fact, one-third speculation, and one-third total fiction—that he was sure would revitalize his struggling career. A mysterious gunfighter, apparent killer of the infamous Diamond Willie, yet who also claimed to be, of all things, a preacher . . . What a tale! Add to that the fact that he was actually seeking Tipton Barth, another well-known killer. No doubt he intended to kill Barth, a speculation Rhoton had already included as fact in the story he'd just wired in. This was his greatest journalistic work, no doubt of it. And just the kind of thing readers of the *American Crime Chronicle* would eat up like candy. Within a short while, his editor would be reading over the story with a growing intensity of interest. This one was a prize, a cover story.

"You know, sir, I can't say I think much of your newspaper," the station master said. "Full of all kinds of nonsense and silliness. Why people want to read such, I can't imagine.

"And you don't read it?"

"Not much."

"But some."

"This job is lonely sometimes. A copy gets left here by somebody, of course I read it."

"Disapproving all the while, of course."

"Your tone is a little sarcal . . . sarcis . . ."

"Sarcastic?"

"Yeah."

"Sorry about that. It's a bad tendency I have. I'll try. . . . I'll be! What in the devil . . ."

Rhoton was looking out the window.

"What is it?" asked the station master.

"There's a man walking back this way, from up the track, and he's got a good amount of blood on him."

The station master was out the door a moment later. He stopped and watched the man staggering his way with one hand gripping another.

"That man was sitting on the porch a little earlier," he said. He stepped off the porch and headed toward him.

The wounded man stopped when he saw the station master nearing. Rhoton was only two steps behind.

"What happened to you, friend?" the station master asked.

"Got my fingers shot off," the man replied, his voice tight. "That gunfighter did it, the one who calls himself a preacher."

Rhoton shoved up close to the man. "What was that? The preacher?"

"Yeah . . . Johnny Cole. He told me his name is Johnny Cole."

A new fact. Rhoton grabbed his pad and pencil and scribbled.

"How'd he come to shoot you in the hand?" Rhoton asked.

"I think he was sparing my life . . . I'd drawed on him. I reckon, him being a preacher or whatever, he must believe in mercy. He shot me right in the hand, clipped off my fingers. I never saw nobody shoot like that."

Rhoton swore with delight, shaking his head and grinning. This story was growing bigger and better by the moment.

Tell me more," Rhoton said.

"Let's get this man patched up before you go pumping him for more of your damned nonsense!" the station master said.

Rhoton, though, was unrelenting. Even as the station master led the wounded man back to the station, and later as he did what he could to patch up his hand, Rhoton continued to interview the man. He wrote down much more on his notepad than what was actually said. Rhoton was a master of embellishment on the hoof.

"I'm afraid I'm going to have to ask you to use your telegraph line again, sir," he said to the station master when he was finished. "I've got to update the story I sent."

"Do I get paid for telling you all that?" the wounded man, his finger stumps now nicely bandaged, said.

"You're building a legend, my friend," Rhoton

said, heading for the telegraph key. "The satisfation of that surely should be pay enough."

Micah trudged slowly along, very weary and not particularly attentive to his surroundings, because nothing here seemed worthy of more than one glance. He wondered whether Tipton Barth was here, somewhere, maybe in a barroom, maybe relaxing on one of the porches. Oddly, Micah hardly cared. He wasn't sure he'd even recognize Barth after all these years, or that Barth would remember him. In any case, all he planned to do was go home and tell his family what a fool he'd been to leave in the first place.

But first he needed a new pair of boots. During this last leg of his walk, the sole of his right boot had begun to flop, slapping against the bottom of his foot with every step. The left boot was in only slightly better condition.

Micah spotted a sign above a store: SMITH'S DRY GOODS AND SUNDRIES. Micah headed for the door.

It was dark inside, relative to the street, and pleasant. He paused, breathing deeply, thinking how tired he felt, and scanned the shelves, looking for boots.

"Do for you, sir?" a lazy-looking man asked, not even looking at Micah.

"I need a new pair of boots," Micah said, lifting a foot to show the flapping sole.

The man didn't even glance at it. He was absorbed in reading an outdated edition of the *American Crime Chronicle.* "Boots are over there."

"So I see. Thanks."

He spent fifteen minutes with the assorted boots and finally made his selection. He put them on, tossed his old boots into a corner, and walked over to pay.

The man was still reading his copy of the *Crime Chronicle.* He seemed irritated to have to interrupt his reading to take Micah's money.

"You enjoy that paper?" Micah asked, struggling to mask his irritation.

"Yeah."

"That the latest edition?"

"Yeah. But it's time for another one any day now. I've read this one through."

"Let me suggest you supplement your reading with the Bible."

The man looked up at him for the first time. "You a preacher?"

"As a matter of fact, I am."

"Yeah. Well, I ain't that much a reader. Except for the *Chronicle.*"

Micah walked back onto the street, enjoying the feeling of new boots but realizing he'd have to break them in before they really grew comfortable.

What now? The train station, maybe. A look for his baggage and saddle. Or maybe not. He was hungry. A restaurant was the thing.

He began his search.

Chapter Twenty-one

He found one that advertised flapjacks and sausage, and entered into one of the best meals he'd had in quite a long time. It was so good, and he was so famished, that he ordered a second one. He felt extravagant, but the guilt was overwhelmed by the pleasure.

By the time he'd finished, the sun was edging down. Micah forgot about the train station for now and turned his attention to the local hotel.

"Room for one?" the man behind the counter said. "Any preference of floor? We've got four to choose from." The fellow seemed quite proud of this.

"In that case, I'll take the fourth floor," Micah said. "The better for the view."

"Indeed. And the rooms are fifteen cents cheaper because of the higher risk of dying should we suffer a fire."

"That's a true comfort," Micah said. "Thank you for mentioning that. I'll be sure to ponder that while I'm lying in bed."

Once in the room, though, he didn't worry much. There were porches at each level, spanning the full front of the structure, all of them connected by stairs. In case of fire, he could be on the street in moments.

He lay back on the bed, napping briefly, then decided to enjoy one of his relatively infrequent cigars on the porch. He stepped outside and settled down in a rocking chair, looking past the rooftops across the street and delighting in the beauty of the mountains, still lighted with the last glows of the sunset.

A splendid place was these mountains. Yet right now he missed the flatlands of Kansas, his wife, his son. He thought about writing Alice a letter, but put aside the idea with the happy realization that, if all went smoothly, he could probably reach home before the letter could.

"Good-bye, Tipton Barth," he said to the sky. "It was a righteous impulse, I suppose, that led me here to find you, but I'll search for you no more. There's nothing I can do about the crimes you've committed . . . and it's the role of the law, not a preacher, to protect the world from whatever crimes you may do again."

A part of himself questioned his own words, but right now that particular voice was nearly silent. Micah Ward was glad, just now, to think of nothing but himself, his family, his impending journey home, the taste of his cigar, and the comfortable feeling of the rocking chair here on this lovely Colorado mountain country evening.

He opened his eyes abruptly. It was much darker, the cigar had dropped from his fingers to the porch and burned out, and he knew he'd gone to sleep.

Something had awakened him, though. He sat up straight.

"I'll beat hell out of you, Starling!" a voice from below said loudly. "Come on, Smith, drag him around into the alley."

Micah stood and went to the porch railing. Below and across the street, a man was lying in the dirt, visible to Micah only because of the light coming from nearby buildings. Two other men were standing by him, looming over him threateningly. It was one of these who had spoken.

Micah examined the building directly behind the men. It was a barroom and gambling house, and he surmised from the general lay of the situation that the man on the ground had been rudely tossed out of that establishment by the other two.

The pair reached down and picked up the fallen man by his arms and dragged him toward a nearby alley. The man kicked and protested, but the pair treated him very roughly.

Micah couldn't see them well once they were in the alley, but he could hear their words, and the downed man's outcries, and the thuds and thumps that told him a beating was going on.

He looked around on the street, hoping to spot some sort of policeman. There was none.

"Oh, Lord . . ." Micah whispered.

The sound of the beating was growing more horrific.

Something inside Micah told him to retreat back into his room and close the door and windows. Whatever was happening across the way was not his business.

Another voice, the one he knew was the right one to heed, told him to get down there right away and somehow stop what could be a murder in progress.

"Dear Lord, help me," he said. "Protect me and help me to protect this man below."

He headed for the stairs and began a fast descent to the street.

* * *

The sound of the beating was loud and sickening—dull thuds, accompanied by grunts from both the beaters and the one receiving the beating.

Micah imposed himself into the end of the alley and said, loudly, "In the name of the Lord, stop!"

They did stop, and wheeled to face him, obviously astonished at his affrontery.

"In the name of the what?" one of them said.

"In the name of the Lord, my friend. I don't know what that man there on the ground has done to you, but I do see what you've done to him, and I'm telling you to stop."

"You and what army?"

"Me and the army of the Lord," Micah said. "Leave that man alone. You've done enough to him."

"Get the hell out of here."

"No."

"You want the same as him?"

"The Lord is my protector. You get to me, you'll have to go through him."

"You're loco. You're babbling like some damned pulpit screamer."

"I'm a minister of the gospel. And I'm telling you, on God's authority, to leave that man alone."

Micah expected the pair to come at him, but they didn't.

"That man there cheated us, insulted us, and

tried to steal our money, right off a table," one said.

"Then he was wrong, and he deserves punishment . . . but if you keep doing what you're doing, you're going to kill that man. Is he worth hanging for?"

The pair of them glanced at each other. "Hell," the second one said. "We were ready to quit anyway."

"You can have him, Preacher," the other said. "Save his sorry soul, if you can."

They laughed and headed out the alley by its back entrance.

Micah went to the fallen man, who lay groaning. He'd vomited, and was lying in it, the stench of it strong.

"They're gone now," Micah said. "I'll get you help, my friend."

"I'm . . . sick."

"You've been beaten. That's what's wrong with you. You need a doctor."

"No . . . just a bed. Rest . . . food. I need food."

"Is that why you took the money?"

"Yes. Starving . . ."

Micah said, "Can you stand?"

"Don't know."

"Come on. Try. I'll get you to a doctor."

"No doctor. Please. Only one doctor here . . . he hates me. Won't help me."

"Any good doctor would help you."

"I stole his horse, his buggy. . . . Sold them. I took silver from his house."

"You're a fine, upstanding citizen, I take it."

"Not . . . quite."

"We've got a lot of stairs to get up. But if you can try, I'll do my best to help you."

"I'll try. God bless you. God bless you."

"He has for many years. Now, come on. Let's give it a try."

Chapter Twenty-two

There were no broken bones, something Micah could account for only because the man he'd rescued was very drunk and therefore very loose and limber at the time he'd been beaten. Though he appeared destined for some severe bruising and soreness that would last for days, it seemed that the fellow would make it through.

But he'd not been lying when he said he was sick. Micah detected that the man had a strong fever. His body, covered with sweat, was dirty and hot and stinking. Micah hoped the man wouldn't ruin the bed and draw the wrath of the hotel management.

His name was Starling Bright. Though hc was

too sore and sick to talk much, he was able to tell that much to Micah, and also reveal that he was pretty much generally viewed as the town drunk in Greentree, Colorado. Also a town thief. Bright made no attempt to hide the fact that he'd stolen many a dollar and many an item from places all around Greentree.

Micah wondered why the Lord had sent him such an unexpected find as this character.

Despite Bright's claim to be starving, he was unable to eat much of the café meal that Micah fetched for him. He did relish the coffee, however, and thanked Micah profusely for saving him.

Micah, foreseeing a night on the floor while a stinking, sick, badly beaten stranger took up his bed, tried to maintain a good attitude about this turn of events.

"Lord, I know you devoted yourself while on earth to just such people as this one," he prayed in a whisper while Starling Bright slept. "Since you've sent one my way, let me do no less for him."

As he tossed and turned on a blanket on the floor that night, Micah wondered how long it would take Bright to get well.

He might not be going back to Kansas nearly as soon as he'd thought.

* * *

Five days later, Micah was still in Greentree and Bright was still in his room. He was bruised, still in pain from his beating, but sober and cleaner. Micah had insisted that he wash himself up, had even condescended to help him do it, though less out of pure helpfulness and more to make the atmosphere inside the room more breathable.

He'd written that letter to Alice after all, telling her that he was well and safe and would come home soon . . . but exactly when, he couldn't say. He didn't tell her specifically about Bright, only that he'd encountered a situation requiring him to give some help where it was needed, and that as soon as he was finished, he'd be home. He told her and Flavius that he loved them and missed them.

Then he headed to the street to mail his letter and bring back yet more food for himself and his unexpected roommate.

He posted the letter and meandered slowly up the street, realizing that he'd not even given a thought to Tipton Barth since Bright came to him. He wondered if perhaps, oddly, it was to save Bright's life, and to give him an opportunity to perhaps see his soul saved as well, that he'd felt led to come to this place. Maybe Tipton Barth had never been the point at all, but only God's mechanism for moving him to a place he was needed.

One thing was certain: Bright was a man with needs. He was a drunkard, a man unable to hold down work, a man who said his home was an abandoned privy. He'd begged Micah for liquor for the first two days, but had quit doing that now, and was beginning to talk of trying to give up drinking altogether. He'd been asking many questions about religion, faith, salvation. . . . Micah couldn't say he was enjoying Bright's company, exactly, but he was feeling a certain fulfillment in believing he was bringing something good into the life of one of God's downtrodden creations.

A loud rumbling behind him made him wheel. A wagon, driven by a burly, bearded man in far too big of a hurry, was tearing up the street toward him.

Micah yelped in surprise and leaped toward the nearest boardwalk. The wagon barreled past, narrowly missing him.

"Watch where you're going, friend!" the man on the wagon yelled back at him.

Watch where *he* was going? For a moment every bit of Micah's charity vanished. He was ready to go after that driver and tell him in far from ministerial terminolgy who it was who needed to be watching where he was going.

But Micah didn't do it. He'd learned to control his temper, and so swallowed his anger and turned his attention back to buying food for himself and Bright.

The wagon stopped in front of a store building

on down the street. The driver left his perch and circled to the rear of the wagon. He removed what looked like a bundle of newspapers and hauled them into the store. Moments later he emerged, climbed back onto the wagon, went farther down the street, and repeated the same action again.

Micah grew curious. When the driver repeated the same routine yet another time, then drove on out of town, Micah decided to see what had been deposited in those stores.

He stopped in the nearest one, the same store in which he'd purchased the boots.

Just as he suspected. The fat man was behind the counter in the same position Micah had seen him the first time. He was reading the latest edition of the *American Crime Chronicle*. Micah looked at the newspaper bundle. Indeed it was the *Chronicle*.

He shook his head, marveling once again at the lurid tastes of the American reading public, and turned to go.

The fat man just then noticed his presence. Grumpily, he asked, "Can I help you?"

"No," Micah said. "Go on with your reading."

He went back to the street and headed for the café.

When Micah was gone, the fat man shifted in his chair and let the newspaper fully unfold. The upper half of the page was a garish illustration of a gunfighter with a T-shaped scar on one side of his face, gunning down a man identified, under the picture, as one Diamond Willie.

A big headline underscored the picture: GUNSLINGING PREACHER, KILLER OF DIAMOND WILLIE, ROAMING COLORADO TO QUENCH BLOODTHIRST FOR INFAMOUS TIPTON BARTH.

The fat man read a few more lines, then seemed to realize something. He flipped the paper over and looked at the picture, the scar on the face, then with a frown stared at the door through which Micah had just exited.

A scar, shaped like a T . . . a gunfighter who also was a preacher . . .

He came out of his chair and headed for the back, where an equally lazy fellow clerk was hiding in the storage area, smoking a cigar. He took the paper with him, eager to share his news.

The man in the café, whom Micah had come to know fairly well over the past several days because of his freqent trips to purchase food for himself and Starling Bright, had a copy of the *Chronicle* in hand when Micah walked in. He put it down slowly as Micah approached, saying nothing and looking at Micah in a way he never had before. Micah had the impression that his facial scar was getting a close examination.

"What's the matter, James?" Micah asked. "You look a little pale."

James swallowed. His eyes seemed abnormally wide.

"Seriously, James, are you sick or something?"

"I, uh, no. No. I'm fine. What can I do for you . . . Preacher?"

"Flapjacks. Two plates, packed for me to carry out, just like before."

"Whatever you want, Preacher. Tell you what . . . it's on the house this time."

"What?"

"Free. On me. In thanks, you know, for all the business."

"Mighty nice of you, James."

"I'm your friend. That's all. I'm your friend, and I want to show it. I am your friend, aren't I?"

"Of course you are. But I don't understand the way you're acting. Are you sure that nothing is wrong?"

"Nothing. Nothing is wrong at all." James forced a laugh, glanced at the newspaper, and grabbed it quickly. He stuffed it out of sight behind the counter. "I'll get those flapjacks right away."

Micah wondered what in the devil was going on. He sneaked a look in a mirror hanging on a nearby wall, just to make sure he didn't have something dirtying his face that he didn't know about.

When James came back with the flapjacks, he seemed even more nervous. Micah took the covered tray quickly, fearing James would drop it.

"I'll bring the dishes back as soon as we're through, like before," he said.

"No hurry," James said. "You just bring them back when you feel like it. Why, don't bring them back at all, if you don't want."

Mere days before, James had given Micah a stern lecture about the importance of returning borrowed dishes promptly, and undamaged. So this sudden reversal in attitude told him that something in the atmosphere indeed had shifted significantly.

"All right, James," he said. "I want to know why you're acting this way toward me."

James went white as milk. "Oh, Lord. I'm sorry. I wasn't trying to make you angry."

"I'm not angry. Why would I be angry?"

James seemed very relieved. "I'm glad to hear it. I wouldn't want to have you down on me."

Micah laughed. This was so puzzling, it was growing funny.

"I'm not down on you. You're one of the few folks in this town I can think of as at least somewhat a friend."

"I'm glad to hear it." James's eyes made a quick down-and-up flicker. "Not wearing your pistol, I see."

"No. Should I be?"

"I'd just figure you might be one to wear it all the time, you know. Just in case there was trouble."

"No."

"What if you saw Tipton Barth out there, unexpected, and you didn't have it?"

Micah frowned. He'd said nothing to James about his interest in Tipton Barth, an interest that had substantially declined to nothing by now, anyway. "How do you know about that?"

James, who did not know what Micah's attitude toward the *Crime Chronicle* story was or if he even knew about it, did not answer that question fully. "I just heard it said somewhere that you were looking for Barth."

Micah was surprised that something he'd discussed with relatively few would have made the rounds of local gossip so fast, or even at all. He was nothing but a stranger here, and surely not that much of interest.

"I don't really have anything to say regarding Tipton Barth," he said.

James looked scared again, nodded, and went to work preparing Micah's food as quickly as possible.

Micah carried the tray toward the hotel, still puzzled and feeling vaguely disturbed. When he entered the lobby he was glad to be off the street. Outside, he had an uncanny, skin-crawling feeling, like the entire town was watching him.

Chapter Twenty-three

A long wail heralded the approach of a train. Micah shook his head sadly at the sound. The day before, he had gotten around to visiting the train station to inquire after his baggage and saddle.

An exploration of the small warehouse behind the main station revealed plenty of interesting items, but not Micah's possessions. He sighed, mentally giving up the baggage, regretting most of all the loss of his beloved Bible. He'd treasured it as long as he'd possessed it, and the likelihood of seeing it again seemed small.

As he walked back toward the hotel, he sorrowed over the loss of his Bible, but also wondered if he might take it as a sign that he was to put the past behind him. He was certainly ready to take it that way. He'd lost all desire to encounter Tipton Barth.

Micah walked through the lobby of the hotel, bearing the tray of food. A young boy he'd seen on the streets a time or two happened to be inside. The boy had struck Micah as a tough type, probably living in a difficult family situation, the sort to be a bully and hardcase. He'd sneered at Micah previously, as he apparently sneered at everyone, but this time he looked at Micah with an apparent combination of awe and fear.

Micah was slightly disturbed by this because he couldn't account for it. As he climbed the stairs, he puzzled over this and the other odd reactions he'd received.

As he was turning the key in the lock of his room, it hit him: The boy in the lobby had been holding a copy of a newspaper.

Possibilities began to click together in his mind. That *Crime Chronicle* writer he'd encountered, the way he'd been mistaken for a gunfighter because of the pistol he'd found . . .

Was it possible that writer had actually put some kind of story in the *Crime Chronicle*?

The thought was chilling. Micah stood frozen a few moments, then shook his head. Too preposterous.

But he would try to take a look at that newspaper, just in case.

Starling Bright was seated in the corner when Micah entered the room. He was whittling on a cedar stick that he'd had in his pocket when Micah had brought him here. Chips covered the floor; the blade flashed back and forth furiously.

"Starling, what in the world are you doing?"

"Whittling."

"You're making a mess all over the place."

"I know. But I got to do something."

"Why?"

"Otherwise I'd be doing something else."

Micah set the tray of food onto the table. "What else would you be doing?"

"Drinking. The desire is mighty strong right now, Preacher."

"Then let's pray. You and me together."

"I'd be a hypocrite to do that, Preacher. I'm not a praying man. The Lord knows that."

"He does. He'd also like you to be one."

"How do you know?"

"The Bible, Starling. It tells us what we need to know. God loves you."

Starling whittled all the faster. Chips flew a good six feet. "I doubt that."

"Put your whittling down. We'll eat. And if you won't pray with me, I'll pray alone, for you to have the strength to resist the temptation."

Starling did stop whittling, and looked earnestly at Micah. "Temptation. I know about temptation, Preacher, and this is something that needs a stronger word to describe it. It's that way with liquor. For a time you can just drink because you like it, and because it makes you feel good. Then, before you know it, it's something you got to have. Like air, or food. Except you want it even stronger than that."

"I've seen it do the same to others. I've also seen others escape from it, through prayer, and through taking it one day at a time. Or one hour at a time. But you've really got to want to do it."

Starling lowered his head. "I do want to, Preacher," he said.

"Then I'll do whatever I have to to help you. I think maybe it was to meet you and to help you that I was called to come to Greentree."

Starling looked up at him. "Do you really believe God himself told you to come to this sorry little town?"

"I think so. I was compelled to come here, it seemed. I just had a different reason to start with."

"Tipton Barth."

"Yes." Micah had already told Starling Bright some about how this journey had come about.

"But now you ain't looking for him no more?"

"I don't think I am. I think I've gotten past that."

"What would you have done if you had found him?"

"You know, crazy as it sounds, I don't think I

ever really figured out the answer to that question. I just felt I had to find him, and try to make up for a failure of mine a lot earlier in my life."

"You said something about that before, but you didn't explain."

Micah paused. He'd not ever told the full story to anyone. Oddly, he felt a desire to do so now. Starling Bright was a virtual stranger, unconnected with his life. Maybe it would be all right to tell him.

So he did. Succinctly, and with full honesty, he told Starling the tale of how he'd been frightened out of giving truthful testimony against Barth, and how, as a result, Barth had gone free to kill many others, including the family of a lonely man who had wandered into Micah's own church, seeking relief from his pain.

"I'll be damned," Starling whispered.

"Starling, I wish you wouldn't say that," Micah said.

"Sorry . . . it's just that that's one hell of a . . . one deuce of a story." He paused. "God . . . you feel guilty, I guess."

Micah smiled vaguely. "You're forthright."

"I'm what?"

"Forthright. . . . You say what you think, without holding back."

"Is that good?"

"Yes. Most of the time, anyway."

"Then I'll tell you, forthright, that right now it's

all I can do to hold back from going out that door and finding myself a bottle of whiskey."

"I see. How would you pay for it?"

"With your money. I know where you keep it. I could steal some, and I wouldn't hesitate to do it. I've stole plenty of times before." He paused, then grinned. "I'm being forthright again."

"You don't need to steal from me. I'll give you what you need, if I can. But you don't need whiskey. You need the Lord, Starling."

"The Lord wouldn't want me."

"What if I could persuade you he did?"

"I wouldn't believe you."

"Let me pray with you, Starling."

"No. No. Not just yet. Maybe later."

"Don't try to put off what you know you need to do."

"Listen to me, Preacher. I ain't trying to play games with you. I want to be different. I want to be the kind of man like you talk about. But a man has to think, you know. He has to get used to things."

"I see."

"I want you to tell me something, Preacher. Why have you helped me?"

Micah weighed his words. "Because . . . it's what I should do. It's what God would have me do. I told you . . . I think I was called here to help you."

"I'm sorry, Preacher. I can't believe it. I can't

believe that God would care about me . . . nor any man such as yourself. There's no man that good. If you care about helping somebody like me, then you're a saint. And there ain't no real saints. None I've ever seen."

Micah didn't know how to respond, and stammered for a moment. Then he said, "Starling, if I'm a saint, it's only through God's grace. And I tell you, all I am is a common man who wants to do the right thing. That's why I do care about you, and why I want to help you."

Starling studied him. "I'd do nothing but disappoint you, Preacher. I'd just fail you. And the Lord. I'd make a show of repenting, and then I'd fail. That's who I am. And what I am."

"You can't do it in your own strength. That's why we have to turn to God."

Starling stared at him, saying nothing for a long time. Then he took a deep breath and said, "I'm hungry. I think I want to eat now."

Chapter Twenty-four

The ghost town of Genesis, north of Greentree

The air was cold, and steam streamed from the nostrils of the weary horse and those of its rider. When the rider halted his mount and slid out of the saddle, steam rose as well from the horse's heaving sides.

The rider paused long enough to pull a folded newspaper from the saddlebag. He tied off the horse to a post and headed for the door of the shack, which opened as he neared.

The man who emerged was graying and stout, his skin heavily weathered and his eyes the color of cold flint. He squinted at the newcomer.

"Was expecting you sooner, Jake."

The rider, out of breath, walked up to him fast and thrust out the newspaper. "You got to see this, Tipton."

Tipton Barth reached out and accepted the newspaper. "What the hell's this?"

"Open it. Look at the front."

Tipton Barth unfolded the paper as he stepped back inside the shack, which was lighted only by the fireplace and a couple of very dirty coal oil lamps. He squinted at the big etching of the gunfighter with the scar, then looked at the headline. His ever-present squint narrowed.

"Gunning for Tipton Barth, eh?" He laughed. "Well, now! That's interesting."

"Who do you think he is, Tipton?" Jake asked. "You ever heard of Johnny Cole?"

"Johnny Cole? That's his name?"

"That's what the story says. Read it!"

Tipton glanced at the columns of narrow type below the picture. He was a slow reader, hated to try, even though it embarrassed him to admit it. He cleared his throat, then said, "Tell you what, Jake. My eyes are hurting me this evening. Maybe you can read it for me."

"Surely, Tipton. I tell you, though, you won't like it."

Tipton Barth sat back in a wobbly chair, staring at the wall and chewing the stub of a burned-out cigar while his partner haltingly read the story. When he was finished at long last, Barth rolled the cigar to the other side of his mouth, gave it a final chew, and threw it into the fire.

"What do you think, Tipton? You know this fellow?"

"I never heard the name Johnny Cole in my life."

"But he's got to have some reason to be coming after you. The story makes it sound that way, anyhow."

"Don't you know nothing, Jake? That rag is mostly nonsense and lies. There may not be no Johnny Cole."

"But it says he wears Diamond's old pistol."

"Could be another lie."

Jake thought about it. "So maybe I came riding all the way up here for nothing."

"Maybe." Barth pulled out a new cigar, this one fresh. He stared at it. "But there's one thing in that story . . . something that rings a bell."

"What's that?"

"That scar. Shaped like a T letter. Something about that is familiar. But I can't put a finger on it."

"So what happens? What if this Johnny Cole ain't a lie? What if he shows up, gunning for you?"

"Let him come. I ain't afraid of him."

"But if he's gunman enough to have shot Diamond Willie . . ."

"Let him come. I've killed aplenty men in my day. One more won't matter." He stopped speaking long enough to light the cigar from one of the lamps. He puffed it into a good flame, then said, "Besides, it would give me a good chance to see that scar, and maybe remember what it is I can't just now."

"Tipton, your eyes ain't what they once were. You know that. If this fellow is young . . ."

But Tipton wasn't listening. He puffed the cigar thoughtfully, then took the newspaper and spent the next half hour in silence, studying the fanciful picture of the gunfighter with the T-shaped scar on his face.

That night, Micah dreamed about Alice, Flavius, and home. The images were vivid, enticing in one way, but accompanied by odd and uncomfortable feelings. He awakened to find a lamp burning in the room and Starling standing beside his pallet, looking down at him.

"You're sick," Starling said. His image swam in Micah's vision. "I'm afraid you've caught whatever I had."

Micah only half understood him. "I'm not sick."

"You been moaning over here like somebody's sliced your leg off. Come on. Let me help you up. I'm moving over here on the floor, and you can have your bed back."

Micah was aware of nothing more until morning, when he awakened. He was in the bed, feeling very sick. Starling Bright was gone. Micah felt too weak and disoriented to wonder where he had gone, or if he was coming back.

He did come back, with food. "I took some of your money," he said. "I wasn't stealing it, I swear. You can count it if you want. It's just that now that you're sick, I figure it's my duty to take care of you."

Micah just didn't have it in him to say thank you. Nor to eat. His food went untouched, and he slept fitfully.

An indeterminable time later, he awakened thirsty and asked for water. Starling was there, and brought him a cup. Micah drank all he could, then went to sleep again. He had just enough lucidity about him to know that he was fevered, and at the moment fully dependent on Starling. This was an odd reversal of roles. Micah wondered how reliable his nursemaid was going to be.

The next morning he felt much better, though he was so weak he could hardly lift his head from the pillow. Starling was there, faithfully tending him and seeming proud to be doing so. Micah realized that, for the first time perhaps, Starling Bright had someone depending on him, and something to motivate him other than his own urges for alcohol.

But Micah worried. His money had been running very low and probably was gone by now. Most likely Starling was now using the money that had been in the baggage of Johnny Cole, whoever he was. This seemed to Micah the moral equivalent of theft, however unintentional. He wished he'd turned the Cole bag back in at the railroad station. He'd intended to . . . but if he had, how else could he have paid for this room?

Too much to think about. He let it go and rested, eager to get his strength back.

It was time to go home.

As Micah ate his supper that night, sitting up on the bed, Starling came to him.

"I done it," he said.

"What?"

"I prayed. . . . I done what you told me I should do. I got myself straightened out with God."

Micah smiled. "You mean it, Starling?"

"I do. I've turned away from all my sinning. I've asked the Lord to take me over and forgive me."

Micah reached out a weak hand and shook Starling's trembling one. "I congratulate you. That was the best decision you'll ever make."

"No more drinking, Preacher. Not for me. I've asked God to take that away from me, and he has."

"Starling, listen to me. Every answer won't necessarily fall right in place just because you prayed that prayer. It may be hard for you to turn away from liquor after all these years."

"But I asked God to take the desire away from me."

"I hope he will. Sometimes it happens that way. But not always. You can't just assume it will."

Starling laughed. "I'll show you, Preacher. I'll show you."

Micah lay back and closed his eyes. "I hope you will, Starling. Truly I do."

As Micah slept that night, Starling slipped out of the room and out onto the street. He prayed as he walked along, praying that the craving that had crept strongly upon him an hour before would miraculously disappear, praying that some force beyond himself would turn his path away from the saloon that was his intended destination—for he surely lacked the will or even the true desire to turn away on his own—and praying that God would forgive him for the sin he was about to commit.

He found it far too easy to walk through the saloon door and to the bar, his pockets bulging with the cash he'd found in the carpetbag. It had been far too easy to take that, too, even though he knew what his secret intentions for the money were.

Surely the Lord would understand . . . just one

drink. A man couldn't throw his sin out without at least a fond farewell, a glass raised in salute to times past.

He had enough money to settle his tab and buy a full new bottle besides. He took it, feeling guilty, praying even as he sinned, but not intending for a moment to give the sin up. Not tonight.

He found a table in the corner and worked the cork out of the bottle. Closing his eyes a moment, he whispered words to the sky and poured the first shot into the glass.

Chapter Twenty-five

The whiskey took over quickly, and the remorse set in soon after.

Starling Bright, still drinking, wept silently over his failure. He'd failed himself, his repentance, his Lord . . . and Micah Ward. The only man who'd ever shown any interest in him or taken one step to help him when he needed it, he had betrayed.

Starling didn't know if the Lord would ever forgive him for this. He'd certainly not forgive himself.

But he could find a way to make it up to Micah.

Starling glanced toward the right. On an empty table lay a newspaper, a copy of the *Crime Chron-*

icle. Starling wasn't much of a reader, though at times he did enjoy reading the *Chronicle*. He stood and staggered over to the copy and tried to pick it up. It slipped from his fingers and onto the floor. He stooped uncertainly to pick it up.

He held the posture several seconds, staring at the picture on the page. A gunfighter, shooting down another man. And on the gunfighter's face was a scar just like the one on Micah Ward's cheek!

This was surely the oddest of coincidences, and it intrigued Starling even in his present impaired condition. He picked up the paper and sat down again, looking at the headline, beginning to read. . . .

It took him nearly half an hour to get to the end of the article, but by the time he did, nothing was clear anymore. The story he'd just read could surely be about no one else but Micah Ward. How many preachers with T-shaped scars and a quest centering on Tipton Barth could there be roaming around in Colorado?

Yet the name in the story was Johnny Cole, not Micah Ward. Who was Johnny Cole?

Starling pondered this question until an answer began to come. If Micah Ward really was a gunfighter rather than a true preacher, then he might use an alias at times. Gunfighters were known to do that. Maybe Johnny Cole was simply Micah Ward's alias . . . or vice versa.

Johnny Cole . . . something familiar there. Recently so.

He remembered. The name was in the preacher's baggage.

The question was answered. Johnny Cole and Micah Ward were indeed one and the same. Two names, one man.

But also two quests, it seemed. The version of the man as presented in the *Crime Chronicle* depicted a vengeance-bound gunman, determined to see Tipton Barth killed. But the Micah Ward Starling knew was a gentle man, a man of true faith, one who didn't seem much interested in even finding Tipton Barth now, much less killing him.

Still drinking, Starling pored over the mystery, trying to reconcile it. Bit by bit he began to draw a conclusion.

Micah Ward, if that really was his name, was probably a man who had to present to the world a false front in order to protect himself. A gunfighter was hunted everywhere he went. What better way to hide who he was than to pretend to be a man of peace and faith?

Maybe it wasn't even pretense. Starling was not a man who understood much about right and wrong, religion, duty, and so on. Maybe there was no contradiction in it at all. After all, could it really be wrong to gun down men like Diamond

Willie and Tipton Barth, hardened killers who deserved no better?

Micah had told Starling the story of his boyhood experience with the Barth brothers in California, and how that had motivated his present journey to this place. But the more Starling thought about it, the more unlikely the story seemed. Would a man really do such a thing because of something that happened that long ago? Well . . . maybe. Old resentments and old scores sometimes had long lives. But Micah had seemed uncertain about what he would have done if he did find Tipton Barth. And that, Starling decided in his alcohol-driven brain, raised some questions.

No man would travel as far as Micah had without knowing exactly what he intended to do, Starling decided. So if Micah had declared that he didn't know his own intentions, that was surely just a cover tale.

Starling reached his conclusion, accepting it with more firmness than it might have seemed to merit in a sober moment: Micah Ward indeed was a gunfighter, but one with a gentle and almost contradictory side to himself. His harder side was driving him to find and kill Tipton Barth, while his gentler side compelled him to hide that fact from others. In particular, he'd sought to hide it from Starling himself, not wanting to admit to a man he hoped to see saved that he himself had a violent and darker side.

Starling took a drink to his own cleverness in figuring all this out. He picked up the newspaper and nodded.

He knew now what he could do to make up to Micah Ward for this failure, this return to drink right on the heels of his professed conversion. It would be dangerous, difficult, but if he tried hard and proceeded carefully, he could probably do it.

Starling took another drink, this time to steel his nerves. He wasn't accustomed to making big decisions, and here he'd just made two of them, one after the other. First he'd decided to get religion.

Now he'd decided—he was almost sure—to kill an outlaw.

If getting rid of Tipton Barth was what Micah wanted, then that was what Starling Bright would do for him. Micah had helped him. Now he would help Micah in turn.

Tipton Barth walked alone, deep in thought, and anger burning . . . along with a touch of secret fear.

He'd remembered. It had come to him in the middle of the night and made him sit upright in his bed.

The boy, years ago, in California, when he was on trial for the murder of that fellow . . . what was his name? He couldn't remember.

It was that boy, the one witness who could have convicted him, who had the T-shaped scar on his face.

At that time, of course, it wasn't a scar but a fresh cut, inflicted by Leroy. But there was no doubt that the fellow would have a scar today. Leroy had a way of cutting that ensured that; he'd always been proud of it.

Tipton laughed. The letter T, standing for his own name, carried around by that fellow ever since that trial. It was funny. A joke of Leroy's that had outlasted Leroy himself.

Tipton's smile faded, though, as he considered the possibilities. What if that boy really had grown up to be a gunfighter? What if he really was such a fine gunman that he'd shot down the infamous Diamond Willie?

What if he really was in Colorado, looking for the man whose initial had marred his visage most of his life?

Tipton sat down on a log, thinking through his situation. He knew he was a wanted man in many states and territories. Yet he'd never been much worried about it, even though it was no secret that he tended to hide out in the remote mountains around the old, dead town of Genesis. Not many bounty hunters or lawmen had tried to come after him. Those who had had not lived through the effort.

He'd made examples of them all, leaving their bodies where they could be found, usually in a condition that sent his message quite clearly: Don't come looking for Tipton Barth.

Tipton pulled out the now-crumpled copy of the *Crime Chronicle* and studied the story and illustration one more time. Would this Cole fellow really come after him? How dangerous was he?

It would take a dangerous man indeed to kill Tipton Barth. Then again, it would have taken a dangerous man to kill Diamond Willie.

Tipton stood, swearing. Maybe he should leave the mountains for a time. It had been too long since he'd had a taste of city life. Generally it suited him to hide away from the world, descending from his hiding places only long enough to rob, drink a little, and enjoy the company of women. Now might be a prudent time to make such a journey. Let this Cole fellow come and go. He and his partner Jake, who had filled the companionship void left by the death of Leroy, could have a fine time in the bars and brothels far from this wilderness, and not worry about sneaking gunmen.

But it galled him to think of running. He'd never run from anyone. And this was certainly not the first time someone had come gunning for him.

Yet this one was different. There was something about this so-far-unmet enemy that scared

Tipton. He was ashamed to admit it to himself. Maybe it was because he was a preacher . . . it gave the stranger a kind of mystical aura.

Barth swore, standing. He decided right then that he would not run. Let this scar-faced man-hunter show up—if he even existed. The *Crime Chronicle* was known for its loose grip on the truth. It had written lies enough about Barth himself over the years.

If this tale turned out to be true, though, Tipton Barth would be ready for whatever came.

In the meantime, he'd maintain a sharp look-out, and have Jake do the same. He wished there were more than just the two of them here at the moment. Sometimes, depending on the degree of heat from the law in the world below, there were as many as seven or eight fellow desperadoes holing up here at this ghost town. Too bad it wasn't that way just now.

Chapter Twenty-six

The night passed without the return of Starling Bright, and Micah arose the next morning very worried.

He was still weak, not really ready to emerge into the world, but he was tired of this room, of this illness. He wanted to get out of this hotel and this town, and get back home to his wife and son.

But first he wanted to know what had become of Starling. The man was—at least allegedly—a convert under Micah's influence. He couldn't just walk away without knowing what had become of him.

Micah washed himself and put on his freshest clothing. He strapped on the Diamond Willie pistol, packed his bags, and walked down to the lobby of the hotel.

"I'm leaving here," he said to the oddly wide-eyed desk clerk. "I need to know what I owe you."

The clerk swallowed hard and looked at the books. "You're paid up, sir," he said.

"That's impossible," Micah replied. "I've overstayed my original booking by days."

"No charge," the clerk said. "It's our pleasure to have you, sir."

Micah was mystified. "Why are you looking that way? Why are you giving me free lodging I didn't ask for?"

"Sir, it's our pleasure. You're a special guest. Please accept our hospitality, with our compliments."

Micah was already digging in his bags for money. But he stopped when he realized that the money was there no more. He looked up at the clerk, then said, "I . . . I thank you."

He walked out of the hotel.

Outside, he sat down on a bench on the porch, surprised and saddened. Obviously Starling had taken his money. All he had left was a few dollars that he'd hidden in his boot, and which Starling had not found. He wasn't sure it was enough to get him home.

Micah shook his head, disillusioned. Apparently Starling's conversion hadn't run very deep.

Well, he had all the more reason to find the

man, then. Maybe some of the money was left and he could get it back. Maybe he could figure out who Johnny Cole was and where he lived, and get the money, most of it anyway, back to him someday.

Micah stepped out into the street to begin his search for Starling. Where would a fellow like him be? Probably in a saloon, sorry to say. And here the saloons ran around the clock.

Micah headed for the nearest one, thinking how odd it was for him, a preacher, to be deliberately visiting such a place of vice. But no stranger than breaking a man's nose and shooting the fingers off another! What a strange journey this had been!

When Micah entered the saloon, it grew stranger yet.

It was too early in the day for anyone to be drinking, but a couple of men apparently hadn't been told and were halfway through glasses of beer.

When Micah walked through the door, one of those men stood, abandoning his glass, and headed out a side door. Others simply stared at him, and the barkeep went pale.

"Howdy, folks," Micah said.

"Howdy, Mr. Cole," the barkeep said.

Mr. Cole? "Begging your pardon, but that's not my name," Micah said.

"Whatever you say, sir."

Micah laughed. "What's this all about? I seem to be getting this kind of reaction wherever I go."

"It's just respect, sir. Begging your pardon for me saying so, but any man who could gun down Diamond Willie and take his guns right off his corpse deserves respect."

"Well, maybe so. Unless he happened to find Diamond Willie lying dead in the woods, like I did."

"What? You didn't shoot him?"

"No. I don't even know it was Diamond Willie I found. All I found was bones, and a pistol that was in good working order. But tell me something: Where did you hear my name was Cole?"

"The story, sir. In the *Crime Chronicle*?"

Oh, no. Maybe that wild suspicion Micah had harbored was true, after all. Maybe Rhoton the journalist had meant business with that interviewing and note-taking.

"Just what does this story say?"

The barkeep answered by reaching under the bar and bringing out a copy. Micah took it, unfolded it, looked at the picture, the headline, the story itself.

"Lord have mercy," he said. No wonder people had been treating him like an object of fear and awe. No wonder he'd been given free lodging.

"It's true, that story?" the barkeep asked.

"No. There's a shadow of truth behind some of it, but by far more lies."

"You're name really isn't Johnny Cole?"

"No. My name's Micah Ward."

"You're not gunning for Tipton Barth?"

"I was looking for Barth at one time, not gunning for him. I didn't know what I'd do when I found him. . . . It's a long story."

"You're not a gunfighter?"

"I'm a preacher. From Kansas."

The atmosphere was changing, people relaxing, the awe and fear going away. "So how did this tale get printed?"

"It's a long story. I happened to talk to a journalist who obviously was more interested in a lurid story than the truth. I didn't really believe he'd write anything."

"Well, he did."

One of the beer drinkers said, "You'd best hope that Tipton Barth doesn't see that story."

Micah thought about that. It wasn't pleasant. Indeed it was time to go home.

He tossed the newspaper down. "I can't do anything about what somebody else has printed, and I can't worry about Tipton Barth," he said. "Right now the only person I'm looking for is a fellow named Starling Bright."

"Starling? The drunkard?"

"Starling the convert. He's turned to the Lord."

The laughter was riotous.

"Starling, a convert? He didn't look none too converted last night when I saw him loving on his whiskey bottle at the Silver Pistol Saloon."

Micah had feared as much.

"Where is he now?" he asked.

"Couldn't tell you."

Micah left the saloon feeling both astonished and dejected—astonished that his simple trip to Colorado had found its way, in radically distorted form, into a sensationalized crime journal, and dejected that a man he had hoped might really have changed was not changed after all.

He looked up and down the street until he found the Silver Pistol Saloon. This one was one of the few in town that actually closed in the morning hours, but a man was sweeping up inside and answered Micah's knock.

"Ain't open until this afternoon," he said.

"I'm just looking for information. Somebody told me Starling Bright was in here last night. I'm trying to find him."

"Does he owe you money?"

"In a way."

"Well, you're looking for him at a good time. He had enough money last night to pay off his whole tab. I figure he stole it somewhere."

Micah could have told him just where, but that wasn't the point at the moment. "Where is he now?"

"I don't know. All I know is that he was talking big talk when he left."

"What kind of big talk?"

"I don't know. Some mission he was going to do for a friend of his. He was talking like a manhunter. It was funny, to tell you the truth. He was drunk as he could be." The man stopped suddenly and stared at Micah's scar. "Damnation! Are you that preaching gunfighter who's after Tipton Barth?"

"I'm not after anybody. I'm not a gunfighter. What did you mean, Starling was talking like a manhunter?"

"Hold on. Let me ask Joe. Joe talked to him more than I did."

The man yelled back into the rear of the building. A tired-looking man with garters on his sleeves emerged, with a glass in one hand, being swabbed clean by a cloth in the other. "Yeah?"

"What did Starling say to you last night?"

The man chuckled. "Said he was heading off to Genesis to get Tipton Barth. Said he was doing it for his 'friend.' "

Micah felt weak. "Genesis . . . the mining town?"

"Ghost town now. That's where Barth hides out. Everybody knows it, law included, but nobody bothers him. Except Starling, I guess." He laughed.

"You don't think he'd really go up there?" Micah asked.

"No. No. He was drunk. He's a drunk, but he's no fool. He'll not go after Barth."

"Why would he have said something like that, then?"

"He was reading in that newspaper, about the preacher with the scar who is—" The man cut off.

Micah said, "Yes, yes, I know I've got the scar on my face. Yes, the story was about me, sort of . . . but it was lies and misunderstanding for the most part. But if Starling read that story, and if he decided that I really *was* after Tipton Barth . . ." Micah turned to the barkeep. "Where can a man borrow a horse around here?"

"Well, you can rent one over at Smith's Livery."

"Cheap?"

"Cheap enough."

"Then I thank you, gentlemen. And I'd be obliged to know the way to get to Genesis."

"Genesis! Why do you want to go there?"

"Because I think Starling did, and I can't have him getting killed trying to fight my battle for me."

"I don't know what you're talking about, my friend."

"It doesn't matter, as long as you can point me in the right direction."

Chapter Twenty-seven

Starling Bright was on his hands and knees, heaving and hurting. His horse, "borrowed" from its place at a hitchpost the night before, stood nearby, cropping dried grass that poked up through the snow and occasionally casting a wary eye on its unhappy former rider.

Starling had begun this journey before morning, heading out while fully drunk. He didn't remember taking the horse, and wasn't even sure why he was here. He was moving past intoxication now, becoming sick and tired. And all he wanted was to go back down to Greentree.

When he'd heaved all he could, he sat up on his haunches and took several deep breaths. Why had he come up here, anyway? He remembered only that he'd had a very good reason for it.

As clarity of mind returned, to a degree, he realized how foolish he'd been. Not only had he risked passing out up here and freezing to death, he'd ridden almost to the town of Genesis, the very hideout of Tipton Barth and his occasional gang of fellow scoundrels.

Why in the world would he have done that?

All at once, he remembered, and almost felt sick again.

"Lord bless me for a fool indeed!" he whispered. "And get me safely home again, quick as I can!"

He wondered how he ever could have drunk enough to make him think he could manhunt the likes of Tipton Barth. He hoped he never got that drunk again.

He was nearly to his horse when a gunshot made him yell and duck, covering his head. The horse whinnied and ran off, over the hill, leaving Starling there alone.

He uncovered his head and looked up.

Tipton Barth, whose face he'd seen depicted on wanted posters in the *American Crime Chronicle*, and in at least two photographs, was looking back at him. At his side was a man Starling had never seen before.

"Hello, friend," Barth said.

"Hello," Starling replied weakly.

"What's your name?"

"Starling Bright."

"Where you from, Starling?"

"Greentree."

"Why are you here?"

"No reason, sir. I just . . . rode up."

Barth said, "Do you know who I am?"

"I think . . . I believe, sir, that you may be Mr. Tipton Barth."

"I am indeed. And this is my mountain. See that building yonder? That's the southern edge of Genesis. It's a ghost town now, but it's my town . . . and I don't take to being disturbed in my town."

"I'm mighty sorry, sir. I'll go."

"And do what? Tell that you seen me up here?"

"Oh, no, sir. No. I'd never."

"I can't know that, can I!"

"Please, sir, you can trust me. I give you my word. I'll never tell nobody I saw you."

"I got a policy, Mr. Bright. I never trust a stranger's word."

Starling's panicked mind began working fast. His resolution to reform and convert held no sway with him now. He merely wanted to survive. "You don't want to hurt me, Mr. Barth. I came up here to warn you about something."

"Warn me?"

"Yes, sir. There's a man gunning for you. A preacher. He's down in Greentree right now, and he might come up here after you." Down inside, something of Starling was dying, suffering. . . . He knew that what he was doing was immensely selfish and wrong, and could endanger the only man who had ever demonstrated any practical concern for him. But he'd started now and couldn't stop. "His name is Micah Ward, and he's got a scar on his face shaped like a T, and it's your initial, sir. It was carved onto Micah Ward's face when he was just a boy, by your very own brother. He told me all about it."

"Micah Ward. That's right. I remember now. The name was Micah Ward. Just a scared little runt pup sitting there in a witness chair and saying he never laid eyes on me killing a fellow. But the truth is, I did kill that fellow. Did it just like this."

He drew his pistol, leveled it at Starling, and fired.

Barth holstered his pistol. "That was a bit of bother."

"You heard what he said, didn't you, Tipton? That story's true, about the preacher."

"Mostly true, anyway."

"So what are you going to do about it?"

"Wait for him. If he comes, we'll be ready for him. And maybe leave him a sign to welcome him."

"What kind of sign?"

"Got your knife on you?"

"Always."

"Let me have it. I'll show you."

Micah had been a praying man so long that prayer required no conscious thought. Today, though, his prayers were deliberate, a continuing conscious stream, because he knew the danger into which he rode.

The snow had begun to fall again, covering up the tracks he'd been following. The tracks of Starling's horse, he figured. Hard to believe the man had actually come up here looking for Barth. What could account for it?

Though Micah, as always, had a strong sense of being accompanied by God everywhere he went, at the moment, on the more merely human level, he was conscious of being very alone. He wasn't sure how far away Genesis was, or whether Barth would be there when he reached it. His prayer was that he would not, but that Starling would. He would fetch him back safely to Greentree and then make his own way back to Kansas, for good.

He halted, peering through the falling snow. Something had caught his eye.

A church belfry! He'd not expected to see such a thing out here. Yet there it was, bell still in place, a carved wooden cross before it, on the peak of the porch roof. A closer look showed, though, that the place was in quite ill repair. The belfry roof was almost gone, the bell hanging cockeyed and bound soon to fall, and the cross broken off at the top like a great splinter.

Micah knew he had reached the ghost town of Genesis. He only hoped, and prayed, that Starling would be easy to find there, if he was still there at all.

He rode on, cutting through the trees and entering the edge of the town.

It was a place of ruin, much worn away by the years and lack of occupation. There was no evidence of life at all here, which under the circumstances Micah found encouraging. Maybe Tipton Barth didn't frequent this ghost town at all. Perhaps it was just one more rumor in a West rife with them.

He halted. There was no sound but wind, the faint rattle of the snow against trees and buildings, and a faint creaking of something moving in the wind.

The creaking increased as the wind gusted, and Micah tracked the sound. Turning to the right, he saw something at the edge of an alleyway, moving and turning, hanging there.

He dismounted, frowning, and drew closer.

"Oh, Lord," Micah whispered. "Oh, Lord, look what they've done to poor Starling!"

He was hanging there by a rope tied around

his wrists. Blood covered his chest, and he was obviously dead.

A cut in the shape of the letter T had been carved into his right cheek.

Chapter Twenty-eight

"Well, now! Micah Ward, is it?"

The voice echoed across the abandoned town. Even after all these years, Micah knew it. He turned, trying to find the place it came from. His hand moved, as if on its own, to touch the butt of Diamond Willie's pistol, holstered on his right hip.

"Thinking of shooting me, Micah? Or have you come to save my soul? Which are you, gunfighter or preacher?"

Micah could not find the place from which the voice came. "Where are you, Tipton Barth?" he called, hoping he sounded more brave than he felt.

"Why, maybe I'm everywhere, like the good Lord himself! Maybe I'm here and there at the same time!" Barth laughed.

Another laugh answered him, coming from a different direction. So there were two, at least, Barth and someone else.

"Why did you kill this man?" Micah called, gesturing at the pitiful corpse of Starling Bright. "What harm did he ever do you?"

"Harm? Why, he wandered into my town! That's no small offense to Tipton Barth, young man. This is my town! I can't just have any old fool walking into it, can I? Right, Jake?"

The voice from elsewhere called, "That's right, Tipton."

Micah caught its direction, and the tiniest motion. Jake, whoever he was, was atop a false-fronted building to Micah's left, hiding behind the front wall, which stood higher than the flat roof, like a solid railing.

Micah kept that building in the corner of his eye, while at the same time looking for cover, in case he had to make a quick dive.

"So answer me: Which are you, preacher or gunfighter?"

"I'm a preacher, Tipton Barth. One who at last felt compelled to come set right what I should have set right years ago, but was scared out of doing!"

"Set right, you say? And what do you mean by 'set right'?"

"That's a good question, Barth, one I don't know I can answer. All I know is, I think my path has been led across yours by a higher hand than yours or mine. And now that I'm here, I want to offer you something. A chance to erase your guilt, to start again. To be forgiven."

"What? Are you preaching to me, Reverend? Did you hear him, Jake? What do you think of that, him preaching at me?"

"I'd take offense at it, if I was you, Tipton!"

"And so I do. So I do."

There! Micah picked out where Barth was: the church belfry.

At least he knew where they were, and where he stood: a bad place. Either one of them could drop him in his tracks, and there was no handy place where he could take cover.

That's why they'd hung poor Starling's body where they had, to draw him to the right spot. They'd probably been watching him from the time he came into view of the town.

"Come down and talk to me, Barth," Micah called, resting his hand on his pistol now. "Let me tell you how your life can change."

Barth didn't reply, and Micah sensed that something in the atmosphere was changing. The banter was ending; in moments he might very well be as dead as Starling Bright.

Who would shoot first? Micah put his bet on Jake, who was positioned somewhat better than was Barth to get in a clear shot.

Micah closed his hand around the pistol butt. "Lord," he whispered, "I cannot hope to hit that man from here. Guide my aim, God. I can't do it on my own."

"Tipton?" Jake called. "Now?"

"Now!" Tipton called back.

Micah had the pistol out and lifted even as Jake lunged up, in view now, and aimed his rifle over the storefront. Micah didn't try to aim. He merely pointed the pistol as he might point his finger, thumbed back the hammer, and pulled the trigger.

Jake yelled, dropped his rifle, and staggered. He stood there, blood emerging, and watched Micah Ward run back toward the abandoned church. Then he closed his eyes and fell forward, off the roof and to the ground below. He did not move again.

Micah, inside the church, looked for a way up to the belfry. There it was—a staircase, very rickety, but obviously strong enough to have supported Tipton Barth.

"I'm coming for you, Barth!" Micah called. "You have the choice—throw down your weapons and talk to me, and let me tell you how you may yet save your sorry soul . . . or you die."

The words hardly seemed Micah's own. He did

not plan them, heard them as if they were spoken by another. Nor did he consciously follow any plan. He simply felt compelled to move up that staircase, without hesitation and despite the danger. Maybe God was guiding him, or maybe some previously untouched warrior's instinct. Whatever the explanation, he yielded himself and moved fast, knowing that this was the very thing Barth would not anticipate. Knowing that at this moment, the murderer Tipton Barth was probably as scared as Micah himself had been many years ago in California.

The stairs held under Micah's weight. He ran up them, pistol drawn, and burst into the belfry.

Barth was there, armed but seemingly paralyzed in fear. Micah stared at the familiar, though much aged, face for less than two seconds before advancing again, pistol before him.

"Drop your weapon, Barth! And get on your knees! You have the choice to hear me out as I give you the word of the Lord, or the choice to die! Which will it be?" Micah stepped forward, hardly two yards away now, intense in manner, pistol ready to shoot. "Which, Barth? Choose! Choose!"

Barth roared and snapped the trigger of his rifle.

It clicked dead. A misfire.

"God is protecting me, Barth! God is protecting me so that I can tell you his truth. You can be forgiven. You can escape the consequences of your own evil! Will you hear me out, Barth? Or will you die?"

"Go to hell!" Barth yelled. He squeezed the trigger again. Another misfire. With a roar of fury, he swung the useless rifle like a club. Micah ducked it.

"Drop it, Barth! Drop it and let's talk, you and me!"

Barth backed up, against the edge of the belfry railing now. He swung the rifle again, throwing himself off balance. He flailed, eyes widening, and fell back out of the belfry with a scream. There was a terrible, tearing sound and a dead thud, and the scream cut off abruptly.

Micah advanced and looked out of the belfry.

Barth was looking back at him with dying eyes. A sharp wooden shard was poking out of his chest, bloody and gruesome. He'd fallen back atop the broken cross, piercing himself clean through, his body pinned on the splintered cross like a bug impaled on a needle.

The light in Barth's eyes was fading fast. Micah looked at him. "You could have been saved," he said. "You could have listened."

Barth's head fell back, and his stiffened body relaxed.

Micah holstered his pistol and slowly descended from the belfry. He felt like he might collapse at any moment, weeping like a child, but once outside again, he simply stood on the street in the falling snow, numb and for the moment unable even to pray.

At last, though, he did pray. His prayer was simple, not a request, not a plea, but simply a statement.

"Lord, I want to go home."

He did not leave immediately. First he removed the body of poor Starling Bright and laid it out safely in a nearby building. He'd notify someone in Greentree and send them up to fetch him. As for Jake, he dragged his body to the abandoned church, atop which the corpse of Tipton Barth still dangled, pinned on the broken cross.

He set the church house ablaze just before he rode out of Genesis. It flamed and smoked behind him as he departed, but he did not look back.

His eye was turned toward Kansas, and he would not turn it away again until he was home.